I0578062

BE MY
Valentine
volume two
A LOVE AFRICA PRESS COLLECTION

First Published in Great Britain in 2020 by
LOVE AFRICA PRESS
103 Reaver House, 12 East Street, Epsom KT17 1HX
www.loveafricapress.com

ISBN: 9781916362833
Available as eBook and paperback

BLURB

Life is beautiful especially when you're in love.
Dive into these hand-picked contemporary romance
novellas and fall in love this Valentine's Day.

Featured stories:
The Curse of Valentine by Glory Abah
She will be loved by Zee Monodee
When Love Happens by Rosemary Okafor
Until Morning by Mukami Ngari

The Curse of Valentine

GLORY ABAH

THE CURSE OF VALENTINE by Glory Abah

Jane fell in love in January, to a man she glimpses every evening after work on the way home. Not bold enough to talk to him, she's content with just staring at her daily fix from afar.

Until one stupid February day when he approaches, starts a conversation and she bolts.

Because February is the worst month in the history of months. And she's cursed. Cursed to be dumped and left broken-hearted on Valentine Day.

Can she break the curse of Valentine and keep the man she loves?

CHAPTER ONE

He's walking towards me, and I am panicking! He's smiling directly at me with intent—today seems to be the day he has decided to talk to me. Oh, God! This could not be happening at a worse time.

I duck behind a fat woman with voluptuous buttocks, and immediately after the next taxi opens its doors, I run in and slam it shut, ordering the driver to move immediately. I will pay for all the empty seats. I just need to get out of here now before he reaches me.

The taxi zooms away, and I breathe a sigh of relief. God! That was a close call. I look back. He's standing there, looking bewildered. A twinge of guilt and trepidation enters me.

I don't know his name; I don't know where he works. All I know is that since the year resumed in January, he comes to the same junction as I do every evening after work to get a taxi home. The first day I saw him, I had stood stock still for minutes, looking at this stranger who had appeared out of nowhere like a dream come true. He is tall, light-skinned, has bushy eyebrows, chocolate eyes, and likes to wear colourful shirts that make his skin colour pop.

God, I have it bad. I had surreptitiously watched him that first day as we waited for a taxi, together with the crowd of workers going home after a long day. That was the beginning.

Over the following month, it became a routine. I would leave my office at five p.m. exactly, knowing that I might miss seeing him if I don't get there on time. And always, I would find him standing there, even when taxis were available, as if he, too, were waiting for that glimpse of me before heading home. Then, he began to glance at me. Sometimes, I would catch him staring, and he would look away quickly.

We tried to make sure we got into the same taxi, and we usually did—a dance that made me laugh at times. When taxis were scarce, he would fight with the crowd and grab a seat for him and myself. The first day I sat beside him, I shivered like a leaf blowing in Harmattan. I kept trying not to sniff too loudly, so he wouldn't know I was trying to breathe him in. God, just awful.

And today of all days, he had actually smiled at me, had been walking towards me as if coming to talk to me for the first time after a month-plus of half-eyed flirting. And what had I done? Run away like a chicken.

From the rear-view mirror, I see her coming towards the junction, the busty girl that somehow always manages to get there at the same time he does. She is also the bold type. While I had stared at him and developed a humongous crush, she had sidled up to him and started a conversation. Now, they were somewhat friends.

I know her from previous encounters at the junction. She usually closed from work by four p.m. and only got to the junction by five or thereabouts if she closed late from work. However, she now manages to get to the junction by five every single day, the same time my crush would be leaving work and heading there, too. I also noticed her skirts getting shorter, her shirts tighter, and her make-up always looking freshly applied.

The other day, she had been talking with him while we all stood waiting for taxis, and then, she'd turned to glare at me and had caught me looking at them with envious eyes. She had laughed and clung to his arm like a helpless debutante.

How I hate her.

Yet, I have left him in her hands today. Through the rear-view mirror, I watch as she approaches him and he turns to her, smiling. The only reason I am able to endure this bullshit from her is that I know he likes me, too. If not, how come he always waits at the junction 'til I get there? Once, I had closed by seven p.m. because I'd had a tremendous work load to finish, and when I got to the junction, he had been sitting under a shade, drinking sachet water.

Immediately as he saw me, he had stood up and gone straight to the empty taxi coming in our direction. We had entered the vehicle together and sat in silence for minutes while waiting for other passengers. So yeah, he likes me, too. I think …

But I am an idiot, a superstitious, cowardly idiot that may have lost a chance with her crush due to a stupid curse.

Why today? Specifically, why this month of February?

The month of love is officially my month of Hell.

While others celebrate Valentine's Day, I sit in my room and cry all night. Why? I always get dumped right before February fourteenth. This has been going on for years, and I have concluded that I am cursed.

***

I'm sitting in my office, tapping my feet anxiously. Five p.m. went by thirty minutes ago, and I am still sitting here, waiting for an approximate time when I know my crush would have left before I get to the junction.

This is painful. I can imagine that busty girl sliding up to him and using every excuse to touch his arm, to hold him by his elbows, to cling to him as if she cannot stand or walk on her own. The thought makes my heart clench, and I look away into my phone, trying to distract myself by playing Candy Crush.

A door swings open, and seconds later, my boss appears.

"Jane! You're still here?"

"Yes, sir," I reply demurely, standing up and carrying my bag.

He is swinging the office keys in his hands so I know he wants to lock up by himself.

I follow him outside, trying desperately to hold my breath. He must have bathed in the perfume he keeps in his cabinets. My boss is not known for subtlety. No. Everything he does is big and exaggerated. He always wears shirts three times his size; he walks with a clacking of his shoes so you hear him before you see him; he speaks with a loud, booming voice to make up for his small stature, and he uses perfume too generously. My theory is that somebody told him years back that he had body odour, and now, he is over-compensating.

As he locks up, I head over to the gate, dragging my feet slowly. My crush should have left by now. It's already forty minutes past five.

"Jane, let me drop you off at the junction."

I smile eagerly and rush into his car.

His route is vastly different from mine, but he can drop me off at the junction where I get taxis from and head to his own direction. I pretend like I don't see the throw pillow he sits on to add some inches to his height, and we zoom off.

Too soon, he drops me off at the junction and I alight, looking around with trepidation.

I spot him immediately, standing beside a taxi. Busty Girl is with him, laughing and holding onto his arm.

Our eyes meet from across the street, and he smiles at me. My knees dissolve—literally dissolve under me—and it takes every ounce of strength in me to keep my body upright. God, the butterflies in my stomach are having a jamboree. Good for them, but bad for me. I am reduced to a mass of nerves.

Abort mission. Abort mission.

He says something to Busty Girl and then starts to walk towards me. I look around, helpless, scared to my bones. If he comes to me now, the stupid Valentine bad luck will ruin things. I know this deep in my heart. I don't want to lose this guy due to some stupid bad luck.

So I do the next best thing. I grope around in my handbag, hurriedly turn away, and start walking back towards my office. I hear his hurried footsteps behind me and increase my pace 'til I'm practically running.

When I get to my office street, I turn back and don't see him. I lean on a wall and take deep breaths, telling myself I need to stop behaving like a deranged person and get a grip. I can't keep running from him. What if he begins to feel that I don't like him back? What if he gives up on me?

New plan: I will have to take a new route from now on. The problem? The only other route to my house would add thirty minutes to my journey home, plus that area is not entirely safe in the evening as it is also known for harbouring bad boys, and it is damn inconvenient. God!

Is all this trouble even worth it?

I consider this for a minute and shake my head. Yes, it is. I really like this guy; I really, truly do. I just need to hang on 'til after Valentine's Day, and then, I can go introduce myself to him like a normal person.

So I begin the arduous journey of getting to the other junction. Of course, by the time I get there, it is dark already. No taxis are available, and I have to join a rickety bus crammed with market women and men smelling of crayfish and unwashed bodies.

A small price to pay. It will all be worth it …
***

The next day, I'm still distracted when work closes, and I don't realize I have walked down to the junction or that the weather has changed until I hear the clap of thunder and look around. I completely forgot my plan to use the other route, just walked down here without thinking.

The thunder booms again, and the rain starts to pour. I walk faster and head to one of the few taxis waiting around. I could get in before my crush appears. Unfortunately, they are not heading in my direction.

The rain gets serious even faster, and within seconds, I am drenched.

Suddenly, a hand wraps around my elbow, and someone is pulling me towards a local bucca by the side of the road. I follow, gladly running into the bucca with relief. I turn to the man to say thank you and freeze, mouth open in mid-sentence, hands stuck in mid-air.

It's him. He's smiling at me and wiping the rain dripping from his face with a handkerchief.

"Hi," he says with dancing eyes, like he is really glad to see me.

CHAPTER TWO

Something unfurls inside of me, my heart literally smiling.

"Hi," I reply.

We stand there, smiling at each other.

Then a voice shouts, "Nicholas!"

We turn around simultaneously and see her, Busty Girl. She is sitting on one of the few plastic chairs that are all occupied, waving at him rapidly and gesturing to him to come. Her wet shirt exposes everything underneath the fabric, including the contours and ridges of her breasts, the pink colour of her bra, everything. Her waving is making her girls jiggle like mad.

He turns to me. "I would offer you a seat, but ..."

"Yeah, there are no seats," I reply, looking out into the rain. It shows no sign of reducing.

"I'm Nicholas."

"Jane," I reply, unsure of what to do with my hands. I hate Busty Girl for being the one to tell me his name. It should have come from his lips, through his deep, lilting voice.

"We are going to be here a while," he says.

I turn to him and realize he is much closer than I expected. From the side of my eye, I notice that Busty Girl is still waving at him while giving me the evil eye.

I nod towards her. "Your friend is calling you."

He doesn't even glance at her.

"But I'm talking to you," he says simply, as if he is just stating a fact.

A huge smile blossoms on my face, and I cover it up with a yawn. Take that, Busty Girl!

"Is that a yawn of tiredness or hunger?" He then gestures for me to lean on the wall.

I shake my head. "All of the above."

"Since we've established that you do get hungry, do you fancy grabbing dinner, maybe tomorrow?"

I know he said the words, but I cannot process them because I am frozen. Like a bath of cold water, I suddenly remember that I am currently avoiding him, that I am also potentially really and truly cursed, that I need to deal with said curse before I can do anything with him.

"Ummm, did you hear me?"

Okay, I can do this. I can act normal. I can say no without sounding like I am rejecting him, right? Oh, God, why me? Why now? Couldn't he have waited 'til next week?

"Listen ..." I keep my face down, peering into my phone as if my life depends on it. "I can't do tomorrow. I'm busy right now. Maybe some other time."

"Okay," he says, after a beat.

I hear the disappointment in his voice, and God, I should smack myself, hard. Here is what I have been wanting since January offered to me on a platter of gold, and I have to turn it down.

"Yoohoo, Nicholas."

Busty Girl's voice intrudes into our space, and Nicholas turns to her, smiling. He looks at me apologetically, then goes to her.

Tears burn my eyes, hot and brimming. I've rejected him. Would he ever have the guts to ask me again? He could move on. He could think I am not interested in him and move on to some other lucky woman, like that silly Busty Girl over there.

I turn my neck a bit and see that he is now sitting on the seat she was in, and she is leaning down as if she wants to sit on his lap.

The pain of regret hits me hard, and the tears spill down my face. I can't stay here and watch this.

I head out, heedless of the pouring rain. At least this way, no one would notice that I am crying.

I hear my name through the rain, but I am not so sure. I only walk faster. If I get to the express, I could get a taxi there. I am already drenched so it makes no sense to stay there and watch Busty Girl all over my man. I mean, my crush.

I hear thundering footsteps behind me, and Nicholas appears beside me, soaked through and panting.

"Why are you walking in the rain?"

"I need to get home," I say, turning away and walking rapidly. I blink furiously, hoping he would attribute my red eyes and the tears on my face to the rain.

He grabs my elbow impatiently. "Will you just hold on? Come with me."

He drags me to a locked phone shop, and we take shelter beside the door.

Nicholas unzips his bag, brings out his phone, and dials a number.

"Come to the junction now," he says into his phone, then slides it into his pocket.

I can't look at him. Every time I do, I see Busty Girl sitting on his lap. Is he playing the two of us? What does it mean that he would flirt with me and also flirt with her? I always thought he was as exasperated with her shamelessness as I was.

And why was he here with me now, even after I had rejected his invitation? Oh, damn! I turn to him. I should make this better, try to mend anything I may have damaged.

"About dinner," I start, wanting to bend, to apologise.

He shakes his head.

"Don't worry about it. It's fine. Some other time," he says through gritted teeth and looks away, placing his hands in his pocket.

His words pronounce doom. I have screwed up, royally. He's no longer interested.

But why did he follow me into the rain?

Probably because he is a gentleman.

A car drives up, and Nicholas waves and beckons at the driver to pull up where we are. The car is sleek and looks expensive—definitely not a taxi.

It stops in front of us, and we duck into the rain from our shelter. Nicholas holds the back door open for me to enter, shuts it, and walks around to slide into the car.

"Oro-Ekpo Road in Ada, George," he says briskly to the driver.

I look at him in surprise.

He turns beet red. "That's your stop, right?"

"Yes."

"Okay. Then it's definitely weird that I have noticed where you usually drop off in the evenings," he says, looking at me intently, wanting to gauge my reaction.

I scrunch my nose. Oh, if he knew that I have also been desperately observing everything I possibly can about him. I know he has a favourite shoe because he wears it at least three times a week. I know his brown loafers are a bit too tight because he walks a bit awkwardly in them. I know he irons his shirts himself because they are not as sharp and crisp as a professional would make them.

I laugh nervously, grateful that he cannot see how obsessed I have become. "It's not weird."

He hmmms and relaxes into his seat, his eyes still fixed on me. 'So, where do you work?"

"Adrian Max. The HR company at Elechi Street."

"Oh. I work with MultiPlat. We're at Ihunwo Street. That's very close to yours. How come we never meet unless we are at the junction?

"I rarely leave my office. Not even for lunch. We have an assistant who buys lunch for us."

He looks out the window, his brows furrowed as if he is contemplating something. He takes a deep breath and turns to me. "Since you're so busy for dinner, how about we meet at Hannah's fast food tomorrow for lunch?"

Oh, God! I freeze again.

All I see are the tears and the pain of every freaking Valentine's Day in my life. I can't do this to myself, or to Nicholas. I am cursed. I have to reject him once more.

And if I do so now, he would never ask again.

"Um, I actually have a … um … a meeting tomorrow," I say weakly.

I dare to glace at him and see utter disappointment and a spurt of anger. I look away quickly.

We sit in silence, the atmosphere thick with tension and embarrassment. And guilt. Maybe I should have said yes, then come up with an excuse tomorrow. Or I should have re-scheduled to next week, instead of rejecting his date out rightly. This is one problem I have—when I panic, I stop thinking. These are basic solutions that would have held him off 'til next week without my outright refusal.

If he thought I fancied him before, he pretty sure doesn't feel that way now.

We arrive at Oro-Ekpo Street, and Nicholas turns to me.

"Can we at least drive you to your gate? I promise, I am not a stalker."

I nod and direct the driver to my compound.

The car comes to a stop, and I grab my bag awkwardly. "So, um, thank you. For the ride."

My voice comes out very small.

He grunts in acknowledgement, not bothering to glance at me.

Heedless of the rain, I stand and watch until the car reverses and then drives out of sight.

I have lost him!

CHAPTER THREE

From my door, I am greeted by the scent of jollof rice on fire. Please let it be Mary cooking this food. Please!

I open the door to my room and heave a sigh of relief upon hearing the clang of a pot cover in the kitchen. Mary, my roommate, should be an internationally recognized chef. Her meals are always super-duper amazing. Ask Yusuf, our neighbour who always seems to find his way to our place whenever Mary is cooking.

The room I share with her is a self-contained, meaning it is basically a large room with attached kitchen and bathroom. She had asked her friends for a roommate to share the burden of rent with, and voilà, I came along.

When I first met her, I thought she was the stuck-up, overly religious, over-serious type. She certainly has the look, with her wrapped afro hair and the big shirts and skirts she usually wears which give her the look of a choir girl or an office assistant.

Until she smiled at me, and I found out that she was the best.

I plop down into the plastic chair with a wet thump. "Kill me now."

Mary sweeps in with a heaped plate of rice on a tray. She drops the tray on the floor and sits down promptly, unbuttoning the top button of her skirt in preparation for the food about to enter her stomach.

Ah! Mary. She never jokes with her food.

"What happened? Why are you drenched?" she asks.

"I am cursed." My bag drops from my hand and lands on the floor. I ignore it.

"Babe, you're taking this curse thing too seriously. Maybe it's all in your head. You shouldn't be chasing men away because of something that makes no sense," Mary says with an exasperated voice. Clearly, she is tired of my complaints.

"Mary, the statistics don't lie. Ever since I was a teenager, Valentine's Day has only brought pain to me. Abeg, I don't want to risk it. After that day, I can meet him properly."

"And what about Valentine's Day next year? Abi, you don't expect any relationship of yours to last beyond one year?"

Before I can wrap my mind around this, I hear a knock, and seconds later, the door opens and in comes Yusuf, dragging in his long, lean body.

"Aha! Mary, shebi I tell you to call me when the rice done."

Yusuf is looking at Mary as if she betrayed him.

I look at Mary, and we burst into laughter. "Yusuf, somebody can use food and kill you."

"Eh, as long as say na better food, I'm game. Where's my own?" He is already sitting on the ground beside Mary who is busy shovelling the grains of rice onto her spoon.

"The rice has finished. I made just one cup," she announces, her gaze fixed resolutely on the spoonful in front of her mouth.

I look resolutely at her plate, struggling to hold the laughter in. There is no way the food would have finished. She is just messing with Yusuf.

"You ... You dey sure?" he says in a voice that sounds as if he is about to cry.

We burst into laughter again, and Yusuf smiles with relief. Mary stands up and heads to the kitchen, presumably to get him his meal.

But she has asked a valid question that has me mulling over it. Do I truly believe that my relationships cannot last one year? What does it say about me that I have never been in a relationship longer than a few months?

All my relationships have always been doomed from the start. If that's the case, why even bother with my crush if it is only going to cause me more pain?

I watch as Mary hands over to Yusuf a plate piled high with rice and two lumps of meat.

"Thank you sisi. I don go sleep," he announces as he leaves, a huge smile on his face.

"I'm serious," I say, bringing us back to the topic we'd started before he barged in. "Do you know I have never, ever, in my life, had a relationship that lasted up to a year?"

"Okay. Is that why you will not change out of those wet clothes first before you catch pneumonia?" Mary asks without looking up from her plate.

I grimace in distaste as I pull my shirt off. "How will I get married if I cannot keep a meaningful relationship for one year? I'm telling you, this is the work of my Aunty Gladness. She has placed a curse on me."

"Why would your aunt do that?"

"Because all five of her daughters are unmarried." I stand up to shimmy out of my skin-clinging wet trousers.

"So because of that, she cursed you."

"Yes. She doesn't want to see any of her nieces getting married unless her daughters do so," I say pointedly, bending down to grab my trousers by the ankles to pull them off. "Besides, everybody knows she is a witch. I need to go to a Prayer House."

"So you really believe your aunty can place a curse on you that would stop you from getting married?" Mary asks in a disbelieving voice.

"Ah, that is where she made a mistake. She cursed me so that my relationships do not last up to a year. All these things cannot be a coincidence."

I grab my towel and wrap it around my body. Though Mary has been my roommate for close to a year, I still am not comfortable being completely naked in front of her. I usually wear my bra and knickers into the bathroom before taking them off to shower.

"Don't you think you are being a little bit too paranoid about this thing? Not everybody has had relationships that lasted up to a year," Mary says.

"Oya, give me an example. Tell me one person you know, one girl that since secondary school has not dated the same person for one straight year."

Mary shuts her mouth.

I snap my fingers. "You see what I am saying? I am not paranoid. That's why I have lost Nicholas before I even had him."

Her ears seem to perk up. "Who's Nicholas?"

His name brings the pain back to my chest. "That guy I see at the junction every day. Today, he came to talk to me and asked me out. Twice."

Mary pushes her plate aside. "Don't tell me you said no because of your stupid fake curse."

"What else could I do? I wanted him to hold on 'til next week, but how can I tell him why? God, I have lost that man just like that."

You might be thinking I am exaggerating about my plight.

Here are the facts:

My very first boyfriend, Muna, broke up with me two weeks before Valentine's Day. He was my boyfriend in secondary school, the quiet, reserved boy who rarely said a word in class. I was doubly surprised when I saw a love letter from him in my desk. He had smiled at me for the first time that day, and I'd smiled right back. Then, we began to walk home together every day until February third, when I waited for him in class after school 'til evening. The next day, I heard he had walked home with Murjah, a Muslim girl in science class. Days later during Valentine 's Day, I heard he got her chocolates and a cute teddy bear.

My second boyfriend was Edward. I was now in boarding school and relatively new. One day in the dining hall, he grabbed my plate and emptied the food into his. We had a squabble, and I slapped him. A senior student intervened and asked us to apologise to each other. He apologized grudgingly, and the following day, was waiting for me outside my class. I ignored him. He pulled my hair, and we got into another fight. The following week, he was standing by the door of my class and used a plastic spoon to hit my head. I reported him to the teacher walking behind me, and he cleared the grass behind the teacher's lounge for one week.

Next, he put a snail in my locker, and I screamed in class. Then he poured ink into my bag, and I had to re-copy my notes for two straight weeks. The day before we went on holiday, he walked with me 'til we got to the dining, and then, he offered to help me carry my bag. We became school sweethearts for two terms.

He didn't return to school the next term in January, and I spent Valentine's Day single again. I heard his parents had moved to Lagos.

My third boyfriend was Ola. We met while going through the rigorous registration process of university admission. He was small in stature, had a deep voice, and always slung a bag over his shoulders like a Jehovah's Witness. He was not one, though.

I teased him while we stood in line for a form, and he collected my number. Then, he began to call, and soon, we became inseparable. If you saw me, you would see Ola hanging beside me, his bag slung over his shoulders. We dated until a cultist began to make advances towards me. I tried to hide it, but Ola found out. He was the fearful type, and I am sure the cultist warned him to stay away from me. I was not scared of him, seeing that I had cousins who were also cultists, but Ola was not ready to risk his life and possessions for love. I heard later that the other guy had made it a point to collect money from Ola every day in school and had seized his phones. The day he left me, he said I was too beautiful and he could not deal with the competition.

It makes me smile now, how that boy had broken up with me using a finesse that left me disappointed but not angry. But when had all this happened? You guessed it—early February.

The fourth boyfriend was Chidera. He was a tall, dark, and handsome boy, a year ahead of me in school. A friend warned me that Chidera was a player, but I paid no heed. I was entranced by the boy who seemed to have it all. He was dashing, fun to be with, and he loved parties. Our relationship was basically a party-hopping whirlwind. Every weekend, we went clubbing, and we would dance 'til the early hours of the morning. I lost my virginity to him after one of our drunken party nights—an event I have no real memory of because I was drunk as hell. The next day, I was pissed, and he had called me 'Janey,' and that was that. Anger gone.

Chidera was the first man I ever lusted after. Sadly, I found out he was cheating on me, and I retaliated by cheating, too. He found out, and we kept trying to see who would hurt each other more. I got hurt the most, when he chose to hang out with his side chick on Valentine's Day and I had to endure the smelly-mouthed presence of Dapo, my side-boy. That was the end of that relationship. It took three months to stop crying every night into my pillow.

The fifth boyfriend was Abraham, a quiet, studious boy who was perfect in all ramifications. He was handsome; he had a very good job in an oil company; he had a car; he was courteous, kind, very generous, and soft-spoken. He treated me like a queen, and I began to dream of a future with him. However, he was not very open with me. There existed a certain distance between us that just could not be bridged. I found out he'd had a painful break-up with his previous ex. I thought I could heal him and nurse him back to full emotional capacity with my love. It would have worked, too, except that he ran into her when we went out on Valentine's Day and ended up leaving with her.

They apologized profusely to us, me and the bewildered guy his ex-girlfriend had shown up with, but I could see the relief and excitement in their eyes. They really loved each other, and I forgave them, even though I spent the rest of the night sobbing into a tub of ice cream.

Then, the last almost-relationship was with Ahiremen, a boy I met at a music concert a year ago. He was fine, but I was just not into him. I accepted his advances because I knew Valentine's Day was coming up, and I did not want to be alone, again. Alas, he disappeared on the said day and reappeared two weeks later with a cock and bull story.

At that point, my heart had become encased in a concrete mix. I spent the last Valentine's Day drunk, alone in my room. I danced around and then fell into exhausted sleep.

It proves beyond reason that Valentine's Day is cursed. Right?

It doesn't matter what I do. February fourteenth has always been an awful day for me. I am jinxed, cursed, hexed, whatever name it can be called. The end result is the same—I spend Valentine's Day recently dumped, heartbroken, and alone.

So yes, I may have developed an irrational, morbid fear of Valentine's Day, of the month of February in general.

Why did my crush choose February of all months to want to speak with me? It's just a week to the dreaded, most awful day in the history of romance.

I headed to the plastic wardrobe beside the bed and begin to root for my pyjamas. The weather is too cold for any other nightwear.

"Sometimes, you can make me really angry. I swear, you are the architect of your own misery," Mary retorts in disgust. She has been an avid fan of the crush since January. Clearly, she is unhappy with my actions.

I pause, my hands inside my box. "Ah ah! That is too harsh."

"Really? Okay, let me ask you a question. Of all the boyfriends that you have had, which one did you truly love?" She pins me with her steady gaze.

I think back. I did like Muna and Edward, but that had just been childish play. Truthfully, Ola had simply been convenient. But Chidera had really hurt me.

"Chidera," I proclaim triumphantly.

"Oh, please," Mary sneers. "You didn't love him. You were only devastated when he broke up with you because he won the break-up. He left you for the side chick, and that was what hurt you, not that he left. Abi, am I lying?"

Well, I hadn't really had much emotion for Chidera until the whole cheating thing began, then it became a game of who would hurt each other the most. Would I have been devastated if I had won the break-up? Nah.

"Okay. Maybe you're right, but what about Abraham? I was ready to marry that man."

"Abeg, you only liked him because he is husband material."

I gasp. "That's not true."

"Eh? Oya, what's the colour of his eyes?"

"Ummm."

Wait, I know the colour of Abraham's eyes.

"When is his birthday?" Mary fires again.

My mind is blank, and heat rushes to my face. "Oh, come on. We broke up two years ago."

"No. You guys broke up a year and some months. You only liked him because he was a good man, a man that any lady would like to marry. But you never really loved him, so don't pretend." Mary is sitting up now.

"It doesn't matter whether I loved him or not. I was ready to marry him, and he left me for his ex, on Valentine's Day," I say with triumph.

"Jane, do you think those men magically believed that you loved them? You have this lacklustre vibe when you're doing something you're not interested in. Which of them did you use to call every day? Didn't they all complain that you didn't love them?"

I stand there without an answer.

Mary is now wearing the triumphant look.

"This is the reason why your relationships have never lasted up to a year, so stop looking for who cursed you and stop chasing away the one man you may actually have real feelings for. You're being an idiot," she pronounces in disgust and picks up her plate.

"It's not as cut and dried as you're trying to make it be," I grumble, heading to the bathroom.

Is she right?

I was hurt when Chidera left me for the side chick, but was all that just injured pride? And yes, I liked Abraham. He would have made a great husband, but my heart had not been completely involved.

All my boyfriends had complained several times that I was distracted in the relationships. Chidera used to get angry when he went for three days without hearing from me. The truth is, I used to forget about him if I didn't see him for a whole day. Then two days later, I would suddenly remember that I had a boyfriend and start scrambling to call and placate.

Abraham was different. I made it a point to call him always, but there was no friendship between us, no ease, no spark. Truthfully, it was a boring relationship. We were so busy trying to be perfect for each other. Usually, we would sit in silence, and our dates were always at the cinema where we would watch movies for hours, then he would drop me off and dutifully call me to inform me he had gotten home.

I was bored out of my mind while with Abraham. I thought the easy friendship we so lacked would spring up when we got married and started spending so much time together. Besides, despite the pain I had felt when he left me, there had been a part of my heart that had been happy when he got back with his ex. That was the happiest I'd ever seen him in all the months we'd dated.

Mary is right, but she has exposed an even deeper problem. Even if I was not cursed, I had never been able to fall in love before.

Maybe Valentine's Day hurt most because all I saw was couples on romantic dates while I somehow always ended up being alone. I also want to have a romantic date on the fourteenth. Is that too much to ask?

But bigger than all that was the fact that I had pushed Nicholas away, for what seemed to be irrational and senseless fear. Nicholas, my very own love at first sight story. Wasn't it magical that he was as drawn to me as I was to him?

I had pushed away my perfect romance story for nothing, nothing at all.

"Do you know that I have lost Nicholas for no reason at all?" I say to Mary as I step out of the bathroom into the room.

"He asked you out twice, and you said no twice."

"Yes. He suggested dinner tomorrow evening. I said I was busy. Then on our way here—"

"Wait, he dropped you off? I thought he didn't have a car."

I shrug. "He called a cab. They dropped me off at the gate."

Mary eyes me up. "And you didn't call me to come and see him?"

"Would you have come out under the rain?" I retort, pulling on my pyjamas. "He now said we should have lunch together since our offices are sort of close. I lied again. I'm sure he didn't believe me."

I lay down beside Mary, looking up at the ceiling but seeing Nicholas' face when I rejected his date a second time.

"It's not too late, na. You can call him," Mary says, adjusting on the bed so the novel she is reading is now on the floor.

"We didn't exchange numbers," I say glumly.

"Then you'll see him at the junction," she says simply.

I grab on to her words, and it eases the tightening in my chest. This is the first man I have fallen for so easily and simply. I owe it to myself to pursue this and see where it leads.

CHAPTER FOUR

So in the morning, I wear the tight gown I bought months ago. I have never worn it before because it rudely grabs my body and refuses to let go. Mary whistles as I walk out of the door. She is still doing her make-up, lucky brat. Her work resumes at nine a.m., and I have always envied her the ease with which she sleeps in while I am bustling about in the early hours of the morning.

Aniefiok is the first person that sees me in the office. She smiles widely, looking at me from head to toe. "Ah ah! Jane, you want to cause accident?"

I laugh and head to my desk.

"Where you dey go after work? 'Cos this gown wey you wear no be for waste," she says, leaning on my desk.

"Aniefiok, you too like story. I no dey go anywhere," I say, dropping my bag underneath my table and reaching down to turn on my computer.

"Anna, come and see," she announces as Anna, our office assistant, walks in with a bag full of empty plastic bowls, heading out to buy breakfast from the street women who sell food in the mornings.

"Miss Jane, you look hot oh," she says, dropping her bag on my table.

I sigh. "Abeg, go buy food and leave me alone."

"She has a hot date tonight," Aniefiok says, and Anna laughs.

They walk away together, Aniefiok asking her to buy rice, plantain, and salad.

I don't usually eat breakfast, so I ignore them and look down at my body. Is the gown too obvious? Well, too late now. I will just have to brazen it out.

When it's lunch break, I don't send Anna to buy me lunch. No. I wear the low-heeled, pretty sandals that had been in my bag all morning and head off to Hannah's. Maybe he usually has lunch there, and I could pretend to bump into him. Or he might be there, hoping that I would show up for our date.

The sun is really fierce, and by the time I walk into the air-conditioned fast food, I am sweating and panting like a dog. I feel the wetness in my armpit and cringe. I walk to the counter without looking around. It must not appear like I came here for him. Knowing that I am about to spend a full week's lunch money on this non-date, I order a burger and salad, then lean on the counter and casually look around.

Shit! He's not here. I feel my chest tightening again and take deep breaths.

All hope is not lost. I will still meet him at the junction.

I grab my lunch, pay, and head back for the office.

It's just thirty minutes to closing time when my boss walks in with our most temperamental client. Mrs. Itubor is the owner of a school. She always asks for top-notch teachers and administrators but wants to pay them peanuts. So they end up leaving in droves, and she ends up coming back for more. On the plus side, we get a regular client. On the downside, we have to deal with her eccentricities and her high demands.

As usual, she ends up keeping us 'til forty-past-five. I keep signalling my boss to release me, but whenever I aim to leave, Mrs. Itubor turns to me with a question or a gist that I simply must hear.

I have been telling my boss to let her go. She gives us a bad reputation, but apparently, she is a close friend of my boss. Pay your damn workers what they are worth. When I first started working here, she had been doing her usual pre-term employments, and I had encouraged my school daughter from secondary school to apply.

After two months, she had told me that Mrs. Itubor basically paid her graduate and Masters workers a little above the minimum wage and expected them to be happy about it.

So I fake a smile, and by the time I am rushing to the junction, it is already ten-to-six. Would Nicholas have left? He has no reason to wait behind this time. I don't bother putting on the heels. I wear my flats and head out, hoping against hope.

I get there and look around surreptitiously. He's not here. I even peer into the phone shop where we had first taken shelter from the rain yesterday, and I don't see him there, either. He has left. He has given up.

For one moment, I almost don't know what to do with myself.

Go home.

I head to the line of taxis and ask the first driver if he is going in my direction.

That's when I catch a movement from the side of my eye and turn fully, to see Nicholas walking and laughing with Busty Girl. She is eating an ice cream cone, and he is holding her bag. They look like a happy, carefree couple strolling home together.

The tightening in my chest returns with a vengeance, hotness building in my stomach and stinging my eyes. That could have been me, not Busty Girl. Nicholas has obviously moved on to someone who is enthusiastically interested in him, and I would spend Valentine's Day in regret. After everything, I would end up alone. Again!

Busty Girl has now latched onto his arm again, her ice cream cone in her other hand. She sees me and smiles radiantly, but I can see the malice in her eyes. She points at me with her arm, and Nicholas looks in my direction. I look away.

"Madam, you no dey go?" the taxi driver calls to me.

If I leave now, they will think I am upset. I shake my head and step away for a woman to enter. The taxi zooms away, and I stand there. When they walk up to me, I smile at them.

"Hi, Nicholas. Good evening."

"Jane. I thought you would have left by now?"

Why? So that I won't see you frolicking with Busty Girl? I smile innocently. "I had to work late."

Busty Girl steps forward. "I'm Sandy."

I ignore the look of triumph on her face and slide into the next taxi in line. There, I have done my part.

Mary is not back when I get to the room. I shower quickly, wear my cotton nightwear, and bathe myself with powder, so much so that Mary screams "Jesus!" when she walks in thirty minutes later.

"Did you go to see a new-born baby?"

I shake my head. "Valentine's Day, me, you, some friends, a movie and dinner. Sounds good?"

"Ehen. So it didn't work out with Nicholas."

I head to the kitchen to make custard. "I saw him with that busty girl I've been telling you about. Maybe he is with her now. I don't care. I am not going to sit at home and feel bad during Val's Day. I think I have been having awful Valentine experiences because I have been waiting for a man, a romantic love interest, to celebrate it with. When I should have been celebrating it with people I care about."

"Wow!" Mary calls from the room. "Somebody is becoming woke."

I pour a little water into the kettle and set it on the gas. "Yes. I don't want to be one of those women who depend on a man to make them happy. I can celebrate Valentine's Day with my friends. Why haven't I thought of this before?"

I pour a little custard into a bowl, add a bit of water, and start to mix with a spoon while walking back to the room.

Mary is down to her underwear. "That's because people celebrate Val's Day as if it is a lovers' day only. No. It's about love. So show love to whomever you love."

"That's why we are going out," I say promptly, heading back to the kitchen.

"Who told you I don't have a date?" Mary says.

I smile. "If you had a date, my ears would have been full by now. Let's just celebrate, only us girls."

"Okay. Make custard for me, too. Do we still have bread?"

***

I head towards the different route when work closes, not wanting to see Nicholas and Busty Girl together. I rejected his advances so I don't have the right to feel jealous. But jealousy is raging inside of me so bad, it's like a living, breathing creature filling me with negative energy.

I had my shot and I blew it. I have no one else to blame but myself.

"Jane."

Somebody called out my name, and I stop, looking around the road. Behind me, I see Busty Girl coming up. She's wearing a white, skin-tight gown that shows off her voluptuous hips and breasts to perfection.

She walks up to me with a smile. "Hi. I thought it was you, so I just yelled your name. How are you?"

"I'm fine," I say curtly.

She rummages around in her bag for something. What does she want? Does she think that now that she has Nicholas, we can be buddies? No way. We have been running into each other at the junction since last year, and we never bothered to talk to each other. She has ignored me actively just as I have.

"Why are you going in this direction? Are you not heading home yet?" she says, still rooting around in her bag for whatever.

"No. I'm going to visit a friend," I lie.

"Where did I keep this tie?" she mumbles to herself, then pulls out a green tie from inside her bag and grins.

I stop, looking at that tie. I know that tie. I know it. I have seen it before, swinging from Nicholas's neck.

Busty Girl is brushing it off reverently. "It's Nicholas'. He left it at my place last night."

My heart shatters. A small sob bursts out of me, and I hold my breath. I cannot let her see me like this.

"So, what are your plans for Valentine's Day?" she asks, falling into step with me.

"Hanging out with friends," I say, then stop walking. "Shouldn't you be heading back to the junction?"

'Oh, okay. I just wanted to say hi." She turns to head back to Nicholas.

I will not cry. I will not cry. No way.

I hold my breath and walk. If I breathe right now, I will feel that overwhelming mass of pain. I need to hold it in, to try and suppress it before it even lives.

Everything starts to become grey before I drag in air through my nose and mouth in relief. The hurt hits immediately, and I just want to curl up into a ball and have a good cry.

I linger on that thought for a while, then shut it off.

If anything, I should be happy. I am hanging out with real friends on Valentine's Day. I asked Aniefiok to join us, and Mary is inviting two girls from work. It's going to be like an association of single girls all having fun on Valentine's Day. Sure, it's not a romantic date, but it's better than staying indoors and having a dad day altogether. Besides, Nicholas had asked me first, so if I look at it very well, Busty Girl is having my leftovers.

And I know she came to me just to let me know she has won. She brought out that tie to tell me, in her own way, to back off her man. They may or may not have consummated their relationship, but I know they are officially a couple.

I might have developed true feelings for him, but this time, I won't give in to the pain. My Valentine Days have been shitty because I have been allowing them to be so. No more.

Besides, maybe this is for the best. The whole tug-of-war with Busty Girl is not good for me. It bears too much resemblance to me and Chidera's relationship. I don't want to want Nicholas because I am competing against someone else. I want to want him just because I want him, no other reason.

I am too competitive by half.

CHAPTER FIVE

"Come and draw my brows now," I am yelling at Mary.

My room has become a beehive. So Mary's co-workers, Angela and Ibifa, are already here. Aniefiok just stepped in five minutes ago, and we are complete, a cadet of five single girls, hanging out together on Valentine's Day, and I couldn't be happier.

The plan is to go see a movie because I love movies, have a nice dinner, and possibly end up dancing the night away somewhere. I am the designated carer for the night. My job is to not get drunk and to stop my friends who are allowed to get drunk from taking any life-damaging drunk actions.

Valentine's Day is not just for lovers. It's a celebration of love, and how can you love others if you don't love yourself? I set myself up for pain all these years back, and I realise that I was never under a curse. I just had a picture-perfect Valentine's Day of boy/girl date in my head, and anything short of it proved a disappointment.

Well, I know better now.

Aniefiok is sitting by the bed, mouth wide open comically as she uses her mascara. Angela and Ibifa are by the window, trying on different shades of lipstick.

I am just getting started, and I am making everyone else wait for me. Why?

I had this hare-brained idea to go bare-faced in a move to further my cause of self-love. Until Angela, Ibifa, and Aniefiok arrived fully clothed in heavy make-up, and I realized I don't want to be the ugly friend.

Mary comes right around and begins to expertly draw my make-up. She is so great at it that I have asked her to make it as her side business, but she always smiles and waves me away.

"Sit still, Jane," she cautions as she starts.

As usual, when she uses a black liner on the inside of my eye, tears run down my face, and we fall into laughter.

In fifteen minutes, she is done, and we are all set. Five hot, single girls.

I use my phone and book two cabs while Mary goes into the kitchen and comes back with a bowl of Golden Morn.

"Why the hell are you eating when we will still eat at the mall?" I ask.

"Jane, abeg, those people can be stingy with their food. They always serve little portions, and it's never enough for me. I will not buy two plates of food."

"It's true," Aniefiok agrees, then rushes to the kitchen herself.

Angela and Ibifa join her, and then I do, too.

We are in the middle of our big bowl of Golden Morn when I get a call from the taxi driver. "The taxis are outside. Let's go."

We leave the dishes in the sink and hurry out. I lock the room quickly and rush out to meet them. Angela and Ibifa are already seated in one cab. I head to the second one and enter the front seat.

Unfortunately, the cinema hall is packed tight. The only tickets left are for the midnight showing, so we head to grab chicken and chips at a fast food in the mall.

"Why don't we go to the bar downstairs?" Aniefiok suggests.

It sounds like a much better plan than going to a club in GRA. We head downstairs and join the small crowd gathered at the entrance. When our turn arrives, the huge bouncer stationed at the door places his hand against the door, stopping us from entering.

"Oga, what's the problem?" I ask.

"You girls can't come in if you're not with a man," he announces, barely looking at us.

"Eh?" That is the only word I am capable of saying. What the hell?

Fortunately, Mary's tongue is in perfect working condition. "What do you mean? Do we look like we cannot afford drinks here? Abi, we look like prostitutes to you?"

She is yelling at him with her loud voice, drawing the attention of passers-by and the small crowd waiting to get in.

The bouncer shrugs unapologetically, as if he is used to women's hysterics and it makes no difference to him.

Rage wells up inside me, and I find my voice again.

"Look here, mister," I begin, right before I feel an arm on my back.

"Oga no vex, I dey with them," a man says beside me, the one whose arm is on my back possessively. He turns and winks at me, and I understand—he is helping us get into the bar.

We all glare daggers at the bouncer as we pass underneath his huge biceps into the cool and dimly lit bar that is half packed. The music is loud, and the strobe lights are flashing.

"Thank you," I say to the man who helped us get in. My friends chorus the same, and he smiles, showing perfect white teeth and a dimple.

"It's a pleasure to assist five beautiful women."

My friends preen, and I roll my eyes and go grab an empty table, leaving them standing there. They come to the table moments later and sit down. Mary glares at me. "Why were you rude to him? He helped us out, and I think he likes you."

I raise my hand in protest. "Please. I am not here for any man drama."

"Where's the waiter?" Ibifa asks.

"There's no waiter. You have to go to the bar to order for drinks," Aniefiok says, and I roll my eyes and stand up.

Great, the bar is crowded, and I have to wait fifteen minutes before it gets to my turn. I order the drinks and wait for the bartender to round it up.

"You again," the man that helped us get in says from beside me, startling me.

"Dude, you scared me," I say, taking a step back. He is standing way too close.

"My bad. So, no special person tonight." He leans on the counter, smiling up at me eagerly.

I grimace.

"On the contrary, I have four special persons tonight." I point to my friends who are busy taking selfies.

He says something, but the loud music sweeps the words away.

"I can't hear you," I yell over the loud music.

He looks at me and points to his ears. He can't hear me either. Must be why he was standing too close at first.

Oh, for crying out loud, the DJ is seriously trying to ruin our eardrums. I lean closer to him and speak directly into his ear. "I said I am out with four special persons."

He turns and says right into mine, "Ah, do you guys want company?"

"You expect me to believe that you came here alone, on Valentine's Day?" I say with disbelief.

"I was hoping to meet someone like you," he says, and I chuckle.

If not for the recent Nicholas thing, I would be interested. Maybe I shouldn't shoot him off. "Maybe."

"My name's Emeka."

"Jane," I reply.

The waiter taps my shoulder and points to the tray of drinks on the bar. I reach for my purse, but Emeka holds my hand and gives the waiter his card. I hide my smile as he pays, happy to save the cash. But this night is not about men. I need to remember that.

I turn with the tray, and my eyes go straight to someone staring at me pointedly. Nicholas! The shock makes me gasp, and the man beside me holds my hand to steady the tray.

"Careful," he says.

I smile at him and look up again. Nicholas is sitting at a table just in front of the bar, staring at me. He raises a drink to his lips and sips, never taking his eyes off me. What the hell is he doing here? Is it a coincidence? And where is Busty Girl?

I look at his table. No sign of her. Why is he here? This was supposed to be a fun night. How can I have a fun night when the man who crushed my heart is just sitting there, staring at me?

I feel his eyes on me as I walk to the table, making me so self-conscious that I almost stumble. My friends reach for their drinks eagerly, and I look at Nicholas' table. His eyes are trained on me, making me nervous. What?

"Wanna dance?" Emeka asks beside me, startling me again.

I had forgotten all about him. He takes my silence for approval because the next thing I know, he takes my arm and leads me to the dance floor. I am all stiff and nervous, knowing that Nicholas' eyes are trained on me.

Emeka smiles and pulls me close, doing the reggae dance that is the rave right now in Nigeria.

I sway my body disinterestedly to the music, craning my neck to look over his head so I can see Nicholas. He's still at the table, but a girl is now sitting beside him, whispering into his ear. A spurt of anger rises in me. He's here with another woman. What about Busty Girl? And why was he looking at me like I was Satan?

No! I won't let him ruin my night. I came here to have fun and that, I shall have. I wave to my friends, and they join me on the dance floor, all except Aniefiok who points to our drinks, indicating that she would stay back to watch over them and our bags.

I sway onto Emeka beside me, and he grins at me. I turn my back on him and twist my body. I feel his hands around my waist, and I turn back to protest when I realize he is not the one behind me anymore. No, it's Nicholas. And his eyes are blazing.

I push his hands away, and he grabs my arm, dragging me off the dance floor.

I try to resist, and he just tightens his grip, obviously determined to drag me along. Fine! Maybe we need to talk. I need to yell at him and get it all off my chest. I follow him obediently as he leads us to a door marked 'Convenience.'

The music is not loud here, and he turns to me angrily.

"Why didn't you just tell me you had a boyfriend? You made me pine for you for months and all this while, you freaking had a boyfriend," he roars.

I gasp. How dare he think he has the moral high ground to be mad at me?

"You stinking liar. What do you care? And where is your new girlfriend? Abi, you have left her for the new thing that was all over you earlier?"

He groans. "What the hell are you trailing about?"

He's standing way too close, and I feel the heat and danger radiating from him.

"Sandy. She's your new girlfriend, isn't she?" I resist the urge to spit as I say her name.

He grins maliciously, "And why do you care? You turned me down."

"Yes, because ..."

"What?" he goads. "Because what?"

I look away, taking a step away from him. I can't tell him the reason I turned him down—he would only laugh at me. Besides, it's too late now.

"You're a tease," Nicholas says and takes a step towards me.

I look up at him. He is staring at my lips, and a shiver runs through me. Somebody rushes past us into the convenience, pushing me slightly so that I stumble.

He reaches out instinctively and holds me, his arm on my waist, the other arm on my stomach.

Oh, God! The heat rushes through me, right down to my nether regions, and I can't look away from him.

His eyes dip to my lips again, and without thinking, I lean up and press my lips to his.

He groans and holds me tighter as he takes over the kiss. I moan into his mouth, wanting more, trying to enter into him.

He brushes his lips onto mine over and over, making me squirm with desire. I grab his shirt and pull him forward, twisting with need. Kissing him is everything I dreamed and more. I wrap my arms around his shoulders and sigh dreamily.

His hands trail down my back, then up to my stomach, stopping just below my aching boobs.

The convenience door opens and shuts with a bang, and my senses return. What am I doing?

I push him away and rub my lips furiously, glaring daggers at him. "You roach. You are here with another girl, and you're kissing me?"

Nicholas raises his hands to his head, his eyes closed as if he is trying to get a hold of himself.

"Go," he says.

"This is a public place. You can't just order me to leave."

He looks at me with wild eyes, "Go back to your boyfriend now, or so help me God, I will drag you to my car and take you home."

His words send me right back to Desire-Land, and my body hums with need.

"I don't have a boyfriend," I say quietly.

"Then who is the man all over you?"

"Just some guy who helped us get into the bar."

Nicholas grabs my arm and whirls me around. "Then why did you turn me down? I thought you were into me."

I open my mouth and realize that I will sound like a cuckoo if I tell him why I turned him down. Why am I such an idiot?

"Oh, you're just a tease. You get men all hot and bothered only to leave them high and dry." His voice is grim. He's looking at me with disgust. "You like to play games with men."

Tears fill my eyes at his accusation. How can I tell him that I thought I was cursed, that I was not playing games with him all along?

He sighs and leans on the wall. "I really liked you."

His voice is quiet and resigned.

It loosens something inside me, and the tears spill down my face.

"I'm sorry," I say with a sob.

He sighs and comes forward, pulling me into his arms, hugging me tight. He feels like home, like a place I was always meant to be. And I have lost him.

"I know you're with Sandy now. I wish you guys all the best," I manage to say, pulling away from him.

I need to leave here. Maybe we can go somewhere else where I will officially get drunk and pass out.

"Sandy is not my girlfriend."

His words come just as I am at the door.

He walks to me and holds my hand. "I am not with Sandy. Or anyone else. I like you."

"But, your tie," I sputter. "I saw your tie with her. She said you ..."

"She spilled ice cream on my tie and insisted on washing it," he says, drawing me close as if we're magnets that must stick together.

I sink into his hands, smiling. Then I remember the girl hanging around him earlier. "What about the girl on your table?"

"A prostitute. She was propositioning me," he says simply, wrapping his arms around me and holding me tighter. "So, will you go out with me now?"

He spoke those last words into my ear.

I nod eagerly.

"But not tonight. I am with my friends." A thought occurs to me. "How did you know I was here?"

"I stalked you. I've been stalking you since January."

I grin and hold him closer. "Really?"

"Yeah. The first day I saw you at the junction, I fell in love with you. I forgot about going to get my car at the mechanic and followed you 'til you got to your stop."

I lean away, looking at him with confusion. "So you have a car. But you have been going home in a taxi for months?"

He chuckles. "I was following you. My driver would follow the taxi 'til we get to your stop. Then he would pick me up."

I burst into laughter. "You really are a stalker."

"I just didn't have the nerve to talk to you," he says, dipping his head low in a shy gesture. "When I managed to ask you out, you turned me down and broke my heart. I was confused. I thought you were into me, too."

"Ah! So that's why you suddenly became buddies with Sandy."

"I wanted to make you jealous. But when I saw your face that day, I knew I had made a mistake. But I still couldn't figure out why you turned me down. Why did you turn me down?"

"A silly reason," I say, trying to brush it away.

"You can tell me."

I take a deep breath. "I thought I was cursed."

To his credit, he doesn't laugh. "Okay. So the stalker and the cursed girl. We make quite a pair, right?"

I smile. It's strange to me, that I am happy. I am with friends and a potential love interest on the most dreaded day in the history of romance, Valentine's Day.

All I had to do was to love myself and voilà, said curse is broken. Because it was never a curse.

GLORY ABAH

Glory Abah is a die-hard romantic whose head has always been in the clouds. She started reading books from a very young age and finally, decided to pen down the love stories she fantasizes about. She lives in Nigeria and loves to hear from her readers.

You can reach her at (cue social media handles and email address)

Join her mail list to have first access to free stories, book releases, discounts and many more exciting offers, including a FREE book. Click the link (http://eepurl.com/dnpV-r)

She Will Be Loved

ZEE MONODEE

SHE WILL BE LOVED by Zee Monodee

This Valentine's Day, the music scene's hottest artist, DJ Den, is set to perform his worldwide smash hit in Mauritius. Jaeden Kang—the man from Shetland behind the stage name—is looking forward to a break and some inspiration before his tour gobbles him up again.

Tanzanian medical doctor Zenobia Hashemi is visiting her brother on the island when her path crosses that of Jaeden and they're off to a rocky start.

Neither of them 'does' love … but life has other plans for them during this trip!

CHAPTER ONE

Zenobia Hashemi had seen her fair share of the weird and bizarre. Her job as a medical doctor with international aid organization Angelos, along with her latest posting at a ramshackle community cottage hospital in the Indian state of Goa, had made her no stranger to chaos. She'd honestly thought nothing could puzzle her anymore.

How wrong she'd been.

She had stopped on the threshold of the conservatory at her future sister-in-law's communications agency in Port-Louis, the capital of the island of Mauritius. Frowning, she tried hard to make sense of the picture before her.

Two women and one man, huddled together with their heads bent over the gigantic table. In truth, this shouldn't surprise her—it could be a hush-hush meeting between the boss and her two major underlings. The five, opened, Jumbo-sized bags of M&Ms would make one pause, though. The glass surface looked like a happy-go-lucky clown had lost his footing and fallen, scattering all his colourful buttons across the expanse.

But that wasn't, by far, the most baffling. Annabelle—Zenobia's brother's fiancée—and her two minions looked like they were playing a crazy game of dominoes with the candy as they sorted them all by colour.

"Uhm, guys?" she asked after a moment. "What's going on?"

Annabelle, a French-Mauritian brunette with porcelain skin and overflowing dark hair, looked up with a glazed edge in her usually sparkling gunmetal grey eyes.

Not good—in her few days on the island, Zenobia would've sworn the woman could take on the world and not lose the effusive energy with which she tackled everything.

She took a few steps towards the table, her eyebrows rising as she gazed at the many piles of candy. Yellow and orange to one side, all the way out. Blue and green to the left, red and brown to the right.

"Do they celebrate Halloween in February here?"

Annabelle blinked. "Why do you ask that?"

She gestured to the colourful little pyramids. "This. What are you doing with all this? Looks like you're getting ready to cater to a horde of trick-or-treaters."

The brunette sighed. "I wish."

Alarm bells rang in Zenobia's head. Could something be worse than a gaggle of kids running high on sugar? Her boggling eyes must've shown her disbelief because Annabelle gestured to the table with a wide wave of her hand.

"Latest client. He demands M&Ms in his room and around him all the time, but no yellow or orange ones. Hates those colours. The bowls should always be kept filled with more red and brown and only a smattering of blue and green."

Zenobia blinked. "That's all?"

The Chinese-Mauritian guy sitting at the table—Annabelle's right-hand man, Daniel—snickered at the sarcasm she'd barely concealed in her tone.

"His room should always be kept at fourteen degrees Celsius, and there should be air-conditioning to guarantee those temps as much as possible wherever he is," Annabelle continued.

"Even outside?" Zenobia asked with a snort.

The other woman sighed. "Tell me about it. It's February in Mauritius. Probably the hottest, most humid month of the whole year, never mind that weather services say that December is the worst. Do we get thunderstorms and drowning rainfall every day for five hours straight in December? Hell no!"

Zenobia was no stranger to heat and humidity. One just had to visit Goa anytime in the year to know that 'humid' was the default setting in that Indian state. But even she was having trouble in the current heavy, cloaking air and cloying heat over this island in the middle of the Indian Ocean.

If only she could've gotten a vacation break in May or June. She would've been able to escape the hottest month on the Goan coast and also the early days of the Monsoon season. Her brother, Zach, had also raved about how mild and temperate the climate could be in Mauritius around this period.

But her boss's daughter was due to have her first baby in late May in the UK, and as such, Dr. Crenshaw was taking three months off—when she never even took a day of sick leave in a whole year!— and Zenobia, being the most senior doctor at the hospital, would have to hold the fort in her absence. So really, February had been the only time she could take a break. Hence her being here during this utterly stifling season.

If she could, she'd walk around with one of those utterly dreadful visors that held a small fan blowing onto a person's face. That's how bad the heat was here—she'd even consider such a disgrace just to be a bit more comfortable.

A cell phone beeped, and Annabelle blanched as she read the text. The woman let out a string of muffled curses in French, which Zenobia knew only a rudiment of, but no one could mistake the tone.

"The plane is early," she hissed. "The fucking plane is early!"

A flurry of activity erupted in the room as the three people at the table got up and started dashing around the place like headless chickens. Then, Annabelle stilled, Haseena—the turbaned Muslim woman who was the other minion—bumping smack into her.

"We need to stop and think," Annabelle said. "They've just landed. It will take them at least an hour and a half to make it out of Customs and the airport and to reach the hotel on the north-west coast." She paused for a deep breath. "We still have time if we're fast."

The other two started nodding, and Annabelle directed them to the M&M piles. Two Jumbo bags remained to be sorted. With this heat, no wonder they'd waited for the last minute to handle the candy which would totally melt and turn into sticky gloop under these humid temps.

"I need to get to the hotel and have everything sorted for the event tonight," Annabelle said.

"Go on ahead," Daniel chimed. "We'll bring this as soon as we're done."

Annabelle nodded even though Zenobia detected a wash of pallor under her skilfully applied blush and bronzer.

"Need a hand?" she volunteered.

The relief seemed to make Annabelle stagger as she turned big eyes onto Zenobia. "If you don't mind, Zayn?"

She smiled upon hearing this. This woman who'd been a stranger just a year ago had joined the handful of souls she allowed to call her by the moniker. Only her best friend, Libby—a doctor working side by side with her in India—and Zach, her beloved brother, used it. And upon meeting Annabelle, the woman who had melted the cold and frozen heart of her elder sibling, it had felt natural to include her in the family she had chosen for herself.

The notion of family plunged a jagged-edged knife into her heart once again. She repressed the shiver that coursed through her anytime she thought of the two other people she shared blood with, and the wicked witch that presided over both their lives. Once their mother had died, leaving her and Zach still little kids starved for love, their father had been quick to remarry a woman who'd had her sights set on him and who'd thought she could wipe away his offspring from his first marriage aside when she gave birth to their own son.

Maybe if she'd been successful, their lives would've been a lot better. But their father had been adamant he wouldn't abandon them, and that had probably been the biggest mistake of his life. Their stepmother had made their lives Hell, Zenobia's even more as, with every day that passed, she resembled her beautiful Somali late mother. Not only could the witch, a beautiful woman in her own right but who was devoured by hate and envy, not compete, but every time her husband looked at his daughter, he remembered the love of his life he'd lost so early.

"Zayn?"

She blinked out of her thoughts and shrugged off the cold and slimy cloak of hurt and suffering thinking of her wicked stepmother always brought onto her.

With a nod, she stepped forward and slipped her arm into the crook Annabelle's elbow, then steered them towards the door.

Thank goodness Mauritian people weren't stiff upper lips. Zenobia had only realised she'd picked up the entirely Indian touchy-huggy habit once she'd come here and she'd had to stop herself from touching the arm or the shoulder of everyone at the airport and the hotel.

Once inside the Kia Picanto hatchback Annabelle insisted on driving—she couldn't understand how a successful and, frankly, glamourous woman at the head of one of the top communications agencies in Africa, let alone Mauritius, didn't have her heart set on owning a prestige, luxury vehicle like a Jaguar, Mercedes, or Range Rover SUV—she hauled the enormous tote bag that never left the other woman onto the back seat and settled more comfortably on the front passenger seat.

"So where are we going?"

"BleuStone Resort," Annabelle replied.

Zenobia blinked. "You're dropping me off? I thought you were behind on work."

"Of course not, silly," Annabelle said with a bubbly laugh. "That's where the beach festival is taking place, remember?"

She groaned. Yeah, that.

"Come on," the other woman chided. "Valentine's Day weekend, one of the biggest music events of the year."

The thing was, Zenobia didn't 'do' love. Okay, she did 'do' love in a bed—or in the shower, or the kitchen, or the living room. She had no problem with the 'touchy' part of the equation. Huggy? A different matter. She had no place in her life, much less in her heart, for the messes and complications of feelings. Only one in the circle of persons who should've loved her had done it. Only Zach, and maybe their half-brother, Rayan, when his mother wasn't deciding every second of his life. But the thing remained, she wasn't afraid to admit she'd always run on a deficit of love and was not looking for any way to balance that. No, thanks.

This weekend would be pure torture.

Worse than Goa?

She closed her eyes for a brief second and clenched her jaw. She was also not ready to admit she might've run from a friend with benefits who'd started getting too clingy. This Valentine's Day, he could've declared his flame, or worse, proposed. She hadn't wanted to be there to witness that train wreck.

So she'd run. Fine, she'd cop to it. Zach had been on her case to visit this place he had fallen in love with and made his home. She had already met Annabelle during the trip the two had taken six months ago to India. So it had really been about seeing the island and getting away from India.

Best not to think of all that. She had no place in her life for love, full stop.

"Remind me again, who is doing this event?"

Annabelle shot her a look she had no trouble understanding despite the huge Jackie O sunglasses eating up half the brunette's face. "DJ Den, Zayn. How could you forget? It's the show of the year!"

Which her agency was organizing. No other outfit had managed such a coup in recent times.

She nodded, keeping her gaze on the road as the car whizzed from lane to lane dodging the ones doing less than the regulated one-hundred-and-ten kilometres limit Annabelle was flirting with on the motorway.

"How can you not be more excited?"

"I'm sure it's gonna be awesome."

Annabelle gasped. "Are you for real? It's DJ Den!"

"Yes, I know."

"No, you don't know! Jaeden Kang. The prodigy from Britain Beyond. The one breaking all records since 'Despacito' with his latest hit 'Chill Bamb.' The music video has already gone over the one billion views mark on YouTube. You been living under a rock or something?"

"I've been living in India, where, if it doesn't have anything to do with Bollywood, it's pretty much not news."

"Seriously?"

"Uh-huh. Tell them Kim K and they'll be like, who? Ask about a B-list starlet making all the Page Three news, and they'll know who she is and her complete bio."

"Huh." Annabelle shook her head, which sent her voluminous tresses flying and almost cutting Zenobia's cheek like the lashing of a whip when it hit her.

Thank goodness she hadn't worn lip gloss, or the hair would be stuck to her lips.

"But seriously, Zayn ..." Annabelle started.

Here we go again. Zach had warned her his fiancée could be tenacious.

"You really don't know about such a heartthrob? Like, the man looks like he breaks hearts for a living. That's how gorgeous he is."

She sighed. "You've just given me the perfect reason to not go near him."

When Annabelle snorted, Zenobia slanted her gaze towards her. "What?"

"Look who's talking."

"What's that supposed to mean?"

"You also break hearts for a living, darling."

No, she didn't! The comment miffed her. Just because she didn't give her heart to the first guy who dropped onto his knee in front of her didn't mean she was a heart-breaking bitch.

"I'm a doctor. I mend hearts for a living," she retorted.

"You're no cardiothoracic surgeon," came the reply on another snort.

If she didn't put a stop to this nonsense right away, they'd still be at it by the evening. Annabelle did spell out 'tenacious' with a capital T.

"Fine," she quipped. "But at least, I'm no diva."

"That is true, though."

If someone had to be the diva in any relationship, it was Zenobia. Not the guy in the picture!

***

Strange how, with a hat on and a pair of sunglasses marring his mixed Shetlander-Korean looks, he could be incognito in this place. True enough, Asian men were a dime a dozen on the island, and even one six-foot-four and towering over the rest of the folk didn't really stand out.

Mauritius might just become one of his favourite spots on this Earth.

Jaeden Kang—mostly known to the world as DJ Den—had left his room when it had become increasingly obvious he'd sock his manager one if he'd stayed. Fergus Macintosh insisted on a list of demands a mile long at every venue. The world, however, thought such irrational desires came from him and not from some fallacy Fergus had concocted to make him sound like 'hot stuff.' Or more like a 'hot potato'—he could see event planners were starting to grow weary of those requests. The woman here, a consummate professional, seemed to have endless patience to deal with Fergus' litanies.

Jaeden didn't have much of that commodity in him after a flight of seven hours from Singapore, so he'd preferred to exit stage left and come out for a stroll.

He let his shoulders drop as he strolled barefoot along the wooden deck bordering the white beach that extended a few hundred yards into the sparkling clear turquoise waters of the Mauritian lagoon. He'd wanted to walk on the powdery white sand that looked like icing sugar. But five seconds on there and his burning sole had protested. Damn, but the sun could be harsh here.

The sounds, however … They were beautiful. The whoosh and swoosh of the water sounded different from the Caribbean. A bit more tone here—like hearing an analogue sound compared to its fully digital version. Swish … Swish … Swish. This was what a calm lagoon sea should sound like. The breeze in the trees—not palms—on the edge of the beach whistled like the rush of wind through Christmas conifers. Come to think of it, the tiny seed-like bits that fell from those trees resembled super miniature pine cones.

He could find inspiration here. He'd been on the lookout for a new sound lately, something to take him away from the Latin beat and low bassy 'booty shaker' thump of his last album. He'd hit gold with 'Chill Bamb,' a retro summer rhythm where he'd mastered some drum mixes onto the eighties hit 'Booyah!' by Benjie Black. Benjie, who'd fallen into the has-been crowd, had been more than happy to collab with him to revive this old track. The result? The biggest hit the world had known since 'Despacito.'

He'd published that song back in April of last year. The audience had loved it from the get-go, the song charting within two weeks on Spotify and staying in the Top Ten for weeks there. Radios had been slow to pick up, mainly playing the track when they kept getting requests for it, and when 'Chill Bamb' had started making the radio charts a few months later, it had been the peak of summer, and this seemed to be playing everywhere.

It had all exploded from there, and he and Benjie had been on the road ever since, at events and festivals all over the world. And now, here they were on this tiny island he'd known nothing about before meeting a fellow artist a few years ago in Ibiza. Guillaume had now returned to his motherland to set up a world-class recording studio not far from this same location. Jaeden had promised him he would check out the sound quality one day, and when the invitation for this event had come, it had felt like Guillaume's prayers had been answered.

So here he was, about to MC the event tonight that would go into the early hours of Saturday morning. After that, he had a full free three days before needing to fly to the Australian Gold Coast for a tour.

He'd chill during this brief respite time, and he'd also scour the island for more inspiration. A music producer lived and breathed for sounds—you never knew when and how something catching your ear could spark an ember of inspiration in the brain.

And speaking of something catching his attention ...

A giggle? It sounded like the unsullied laughter of a five-year-old wee lassie who'd just discovered the meaning of happiness.

A massive tent had been erected farther ahead. Standard procedure before an event—the technical team would be setting up the equipment and sound system from under there and doing the sound checks. If the weather stayed clear, they'd remove the tent, and the event would take place in the open outdoors. With any forecast of rain—checked last-minute—the roof of the tent would remain with the side flaps brought up. Terrible for sound quality, but electric stuff and rain did not mix. He crossed his fingers there'd be no rain expected for tonight.

He'd been going to the tent with the intent of checking out the mixing equipment they'd set out for him to use that night. Never mind that he usually sent detailed and accurate specs the organizers were supposed to meet to the latest nth degree. You just never knew what you were going to end up with. He'd once done a show where, at the last minute, he'd found out the dial for the video effects he would've played with alongside the tracks had not been working.

Thank goodness he dealt mostly in music and sounds, though. Music, to him, had always been the creation of beauty using instruments and voice. Give him that, and he was a happy camper. Anything else amounted to bells and whistles. His job was to create a mood and make people dance, to raise their vibration and make them have a good time—more so during live events like this.

But this sound he'd just heard ... Where had it come from?

For the first time in his life ever since he'd started performing, he didn't make a beeline for the stage when he lifted the flap of the tent and ducked inside. After removing his sunglasses, he could see with a quick glance they hadn't made the error of putting a turntable up there—that had happened once, the people not knowing that all DJs didn't simply move their hands and scratch vinyl; he'd never really done vinyl, to be honest.

No, he matched Beats Per Minute, finding the perfect BPM to mix one song into another seamlessly and at the same time heighten the experience of the audience. He worked with changing speeds, adjusting EQ and Key. Sometimes, when the location afforded the possibility, he mixed in visuals such as lights and audio effects to some tracks. His job was to make the crowd go wild, and he did it well—he knew that.

The people here seemed professional enough; he was pretty sure no nasty surprise waited at the DJ booth.

Now for the real surprise he wanted to uncover. Who would let a five-year-old around this kind of setting? Stranger things had happened. If he could replicate the joy in that sound—

And there it was again!

His keen ears focalized on the giggle and pinpointed it to a far end of the tent. He turned in that direction, his feet already taking steps towards where this girl must be. First, to find her responsible party and make sure the person knew Jaeden wasn't a creep. Then, if he had to bribe this lass with ice cream—with the parent's permission, of course—and push her on a swing all day to get her to giggle like this, he would do it. Everything in him wanted to find that sound and treasure it like an archaeologist would unearth a priceless relic and remain in awe in its presence.

He heard a voice. A garbled sound which he knew was English yet sounded anything but. That's what everyone who heard Benjie Black's drawling Jamaican accent said. Only the man himself seemed to understand what he uttered. Jaeden had always thought Scottish and northern people took the cake there—himself being from Shetland, he'd had to work on his accent to make it understandable down south and then across the world—but Benjie took an incomprehensible accent to another level.

His gaze alighted on the pale-skinned, sixty-something Lothario with the blond Afro and whose head was bent as he kissed the back of a woman's hand. Women flocked to him like bees to honey, that one. Not that Jaeden had to complain about his own appeal, but Benjie had that effortless special something that made him a sympathetic cad.

And that giggle came again!

From the woman whose hand Benjie was kissing.

And she looks nothing like a five-year-old! She was a woman, all right, definitely legal. Though not too tall, statuesque would be the word he'd use to describe her. She carried herself like a regal queen, and upon seeing the rich caramel tone of her polished skin and the long, black braids that trailed all the way to the small of her back, he could easily imagine her on a throne somewhere in an ancient land like Nubia or Abyssinia.

A ray of sun touched her from the clear flap in the roof, highlighting her complexion with a golden glow that further emphasized that she had to be of mixed heritage—Black and White, most probably. She brought to mind a heather pixie, making him think of siths and faeries.

And when she turned her dainty head just this way and the light caught her eyes, his legs faltered. For she had the most beautiful green eyes like pools of jade someone would get lost in if they stared into those sparkly irises for too long.

Who is she?

The first thing he did was glance at her left hand, in clear view at her side. No hint of metal on there, so not married. He might go after beautiful women but never ones that were married.

Fair game!

She had an official-looking lanyard dangling from her neck. She must be working on the event. He wasn't averse to mixing business with pleasure, and the more he stared at her, the more he became convinced she had to be a woman who knew what she wanted and who wouldn't be expecting roses and champagne beyond the hours of a fling. That hardness in those jade eyes? Yes, he'd seen them with the slant of a sunray. Still not enough to make him keep his distance. In fact, he grew more entranced.

Benjie finally released her right hand, and another giggle settled as a soft smile on her beautiful face with the delicate features just sharp enough to make one realise she was a living and breathing woman and not a perfect statue.

She listened patiently to the man's suave request that they have dinner later, to which she laughed and shook her head. Benjie appeared deflated but recovered quickly enough to mutter some gibberish as to how, if he were allowed in her beautiful radiance, he'd die a happy man.

She seemed about to laugh again, but she tilted her head just this way and saw Jaeden. Her face froze, then a scowl settled on there. Her thick, arched brows furrowed, and she placed a quick hand on Benjie's shoulder, asking to be excused. Next, she stalked his way with long, loping steps despite wearing flip flops and not high heels as one would expect with such a determined gait.

"I'm sorry, you cannot be in here," she chided once she'd drawn close enough.

Jaeden had to pause and blink at the conviction in her voice. "Aye?"

"Yes?"

"What?" he asked, now confused.

She shook her head, which sent her braids swishing side to side. "What were you going to say?"

"Me? Nothing." He'd been too flabbergasted to even form a reply, let alone speak it out.

"You said 'I ...' and left it dangling."

He frowned. What was she on about? Then it caught him. Phonetically, that did sound like what he'd said.

"No, I meant ..." Upon seeing the blank look on her face turn to something like anger as her eyes clouded over, he took a step back, both literally and figuratively. "What do you mean, I can't be here? Is it a surprise or something?"

"Sir, you're not wearing a pass. Only those with a pass can be here right now. If you're interested in the show, please come by later when it is about to start. You can't be here now."

Bloody lanyard. He'd left it in his room. Who in their right mind would ask him for a pass, when he was the star of the night?

This woman, for starters.

"Listen—" he started.

"Sir, I'm gonna have to ask security to escort you out."

At a loss for words, he simply stared at her. Up close, she appeared to be a full foot shorter than him, or just about. In her white Lacoste dress, she looked like she'd just come from the tennis lawn after a leisurely game. Still, the ferocity on her face belied that casual picture as she stood there completely nonplussed and going toe to toe with him.

Jaeden heard a guffaw, and he looked to the side to find Benjie leaning against the stage and having a good laugh at his expense. The wink the older man sent him told him he was on his own as Benjie was enjoying the show way too much. Women usually threw themselves at him the second they glimpsed him, yet this one seemed to have no clue about his identity.

Maybe she couldn't see him properly. He removed his hat and ruffled his hair which had flattened out.

She gave an audible gasp, and he smiled. So she'd recognized him. Finally. He wasn't a jerk—really, he wasn't—but he wouldn't be averse to milking this for all its worth. To earn her pardon, he would get her to have a drink with him later. And if that led to more … well, he knew how to play his cards.

She shook her head and glanced around before bringing her green gaze back on him.

"Sir, I'm afraid without a pass, you cannot be here …"

Her voice sounded less vehement than before, but she still seemed hell-bent on throwing him out of his own event.

Flabbergasted, he stood there, gaping at her. "You have no idea who I am, do you?"

He'd swear, when she straightened her spine in reaction to his words, she grew taller by a few inches. The look on her face also darkened, her full lips now pursed.

"If you think you being a pretty boy should open all the doors for you, especially with women, you have another think coming," she threw out.

At least she thought him pretty. But she hadn't figured out his identity. And if that hadn't happened by now, it wouldn't happen anytime soon. Without being told so over and over in his life, even he knew he had a very distinctive face someone would probably remember if they had seen it before. It wasn't often the combination of a Korean father's Asian looks mingled with the pixie Scottish/Norse heritage of his mother's side of the family.

"Listen, why don't we have a drink and we can settle this? I'm—"

"Not interested in who you are or having a drink with you. Sorry, not sorry." She gestured towards the door. "Please leave before I have security escort you out."

Benjie was in stitches by now, holding on to his ribs as tears spilled from his eyes, so much he was laughing.

"Help me out here, aye?" he asked his collaborator who had also become a friend along the way.

An even more garbled yarp came from Benjie as he tried to speak through the laughter. No help would come from there. He glanced around the room. One of the many lads hauling stuff around must know who he was, surely. Hell, even the security guys must know his identity.

"Mr. Kang! There you are," trilled the lilting voice that spoke English with a curling edge of French—Annabelle de Castelban, the woman behind this whole trip, came from French-Mauritian stock. He'd already figured they spoke both English and French with a different audio connotation than the rest of Mauritians.

He turned towards the beautiful brunette who looked deceptively amenable but who clearly meant business. He'd liked that about her, hence the reason he'd accepted her offer to come to this event when he'd turned down a few other proposals from agencies on this island.

"Jaeden, please," he told her with a smile.

She blushed prettily. "Jaeden, sure. Oh, I see you two have met already. I so wanted to introduce you, but never mind."

It lay on the tip of his tongue to tell her to please proceed with the introductions, but one look at the jade-eyed sith made him bite said tongue. She seemed to have some beef against him, and he didn't do complicated women. Too ... well, complicated.

"So, Jaeden," Annabelle continued. "I've gone over the list of your requirements once more with Mr. Macintosh, and I'm pretty sure we've got it all covered."

He'd grant her this—her competence couldn't be questioned. But his acute hearing did pick the slight falter in her tone when she spoke of the list and the pending hope it was all taken care of.

Still, something else caught his attention. A soft snort, and frankly, even that sounded beautiful. On par with the giggle, because both had come from the same woman.

She shook her head, pursed her lips, and brushed past them, asking to be excused.

He was sure she hadn't meant for him to hear the next word, but he heard it nevertheless.

Diva, she'd said.

Damn Fergus!

Far from him to even want to chase after huffy ice queens, but this woman had sparked something in him. And because of his manager, he had lost his chance with her before he'd even made her acquaintance.

Damn it!

CHAPTER TWO

The next day, Jaeden elected to join a group tour Annabelle had planned for his crew. He'd been all set to board the coach that would take them inland towards the indigenous forests in the Black River Gorges National Park. After four hours of sleep, he'd thought he might nap a little on the trip from the north of the island where they were residing to the south-west and the forest area.

Nine o'clock chimed, and there he was at Reception to meet the rest of the team. He was making a beeline for Annabelle when his manager cut across and steered him in the other direction. Turned out Fergus had arranged for a private car to take them to the site, his reasoning being that the bus would be too crowded and stuffy for Jaeden who needed his cooler temps at all times.

He should've put his foot down at this point, but he knew which battles to pick and fight with Fergus. The man was increasingly becoming a pain in his backside, and lately, he'd been asking himself if it wouldn't be better for them to cut ties. But Fergus had been with him from his earliest days in the business. When Britain Beyond, the boy band of four lads from Shetland, Scotland, Wales, and Northern Ireland that had given him his break into the music scene, had quietly imploded, Fergus had been his rock. Jaeden had been all of eighteen at the time. Almost ten years with someone—loyalty had to count for something, right?

So he blipped the raving lunacies of the Scotsman and settled for the car trip to the national reserve. He did have to admit that the almost Arctic AC in the vehicle helped soothe him and bring his tired body some more rest.

When they alighted on the asphalted parking lot at the top of the gorges, the coach bus hadn't yet arrived. However, Fergus had arranged for a private guide for the two of them, and Jaeden meekly followed as they descended a flight of steps and merged right into the verdant forest sloping on the sides of this canyon-like crevasse.

The guide droned on and on about local endemic plants and how indigenous birds had been brought back from the brink of extinction to populate these forests again. The man had forgotten to add that mosquitoes also enjoyed a paradisiac life under those green canopies. As Fergus battled yet again with a cloud of buzzing insects around him, Jaeden took that as his opportunity to break from the pack and set out a little farther into the woodland.

And there it was. Silence, broken by the trill of birds the kind he'd never heard before. The long streaks of ferns and other shrubs close to the ground rustled as he walked through them, and he could almost imagine the sun, as it peaked through the cover of leaves and branches, playing a symphonic peek-a-boo with him.

Inspiration. He'd been right that he would find it here. Nature always delivered and gave to an artist. The very air in this place smelled different, a freshness that reminded him of cool and humid Shetland while retaining the specific pungency of woods with plant life in all stages of life from blossoming to decay.

Jaeden closed his eyes and slowly turned in a circle with his arms extended. It felt like a sound bath in novel yet familiar surroundings, something infusing his soul with energy and vibrating radiance. God, he'd missed Nature. He never reckoned just how much until he immersed himself in its beauty and uncomplicated giving again.

He listened to the sounds the birds made. The coos and tweets settled into a pattern in his mind, then the swish … swish … swish … of the calm lagoons here placed itself on top. In the back of his head, a few notes of the fiddle started to accord themselves to the bird sound and mix and merge into a new rhythm that fired his blood.

That's it!

That was the sound he'd been looking for. His first album had paid homage to Shetland music. He hadn't worked with fiddle and traditional notes ever since. Something in his heart had told him he'd have to go back to his roots now to find new inspiration, but he'd also needed to mix old with new, with fresh and unusual, and this island's indigenous reserve had just given him that.

He couldn't wait to get back to his room where he'd put together this loop. Paul, his best mate and the only pro-mixing engineer he allowed to touch his music, would love it when he reviewed it later. He had found the starting block he'd needed.

Time stopped as he let himself take in all this auditory raw material, and when he opened his eyes, he caught himself lurching to the side. He'd probably been spinning in place for a while. He blinked as he tried to find his bearing again. Strange how he didn't recognize the trees and the fern fronds around here. He could now also see five-foot-tall bushes with dry-looking, spindly branches and gleaming red fruits like oversized berries growing on them.

Wait a second. He must've strayed a bit farther off from the guide and Fergus. Sunlight peeked from a few branches just up ahead. It looked like a clearing of some sort. Maybe he'd find a landmark or some other identifiable point from there and be able to join his group or even the one Annabelle must be leading.

He started in the direction of the sun rays, but guess he'd been spinning for way longer than he'd thought. His body lurched, and as he caught himself, his foot landed into nothingness, and he lost his equilibrium. Falling into a sitting position on his buttocks, he tried to grab a hanging vine but failed miserably when something tore at the skin of his calf and the pain made him curse aloud.

The tree came at him way too quickly, and he could only close his eyes and lift his arms before impact.

***

That's how hiking should be done: in silence, preferably alone, unless the other person or the rest of the party could keep their mouths shut.

Zenobia adjusted the straps of her backpack and assessed the slope that would take her down into the belly of the canyon-like gorges. True enough, all the spectacular vistas would be visible when one climbed up, but she wasn't one for the big picture in anything. Give her a solitary, one-on-one, immersive experience, and her little heart would sing. Zach knew of her skills as a hiker because he'd taught her. Her brother had thus convinced Annabelle that Zenobia could set out on her own well before everyone else and she'd then meet them to take the bus back to the hotel.

Also, frankly, they were on a tiny island, and this park encompassed only a few thousand hectares of forest. If someone knew what they were doing, it would take them no more than half a day to cross from one point to the other and emerge out.

The sunlight dipping through the branches and leaves seemed to suddenly dim. While grateful that she wouldn't have to apply sunscreen again, it did make her worry. Both Zach and Annabelle had told her February was the unofficial month for bracing thunderstorms that brought rain which would pound for hours at an end. Was she getting caught in that dreadful loop?

Going back the way she had come, the option making the most sense, would take her another two hours of trekking. If she'd calculated right based on their trip here, the main road in this area followed the forest and the ridge of the slope to her left. When she climbed her way up, at some point, she'd end up on that asphalted route and could then find her way to a village or to the parking lot where the bus that had brought the rest of the expedition awaited.

Facing a thunderous downpour on a roadside would prove much better than amid all those trees. She also hated thunder, a total chicken about it.

As she started left and drew closer to a clearing at the very bottom of the gorges, crunching, shuffling sounds caught her attention. Cripes. They'd been told wild boars roamed the forests on the island. Would she encounter one? Or, it could be a deer. If she recalled right, this park was a no-hunting zone. Even though she'd read that hunting season ran from June to September, she preferred not to take her chances.

She would definitely have to go across the clearing to the other side. Guess she'd have to do it as stealthily as possible to not disturb the wildlife.

Zenobia, however, blinked as she emerged into the open. Because it wasn't a deer or a boar out there, though the latter proved debatable. No way wouldn't she recognize this man now that she'd laid eyes on him the previous day. The athletic build, those massive shoulders, the long and muscled legs, all with the face of a manga prince who looked like he broke hearts for a living, definitely.

What was Jaeden Kang doing out here? And how the hell did he hope he would find a signal in the middle of nowhere like this, never mind how much he waved his phone in the air with his long arms extended?

Clouds were gathering, dimming the light further and making a cloak like that of twilight fall over the forest. But she could still see his light-coloured clothes and how the hem on the right leg of his Bermuda shorts looked a ragged, uneven dark brown.

Something sounded the alarm in her head, and she squinted. The pale gold skin of his calf also sported the same stain, but redder.

Blood. He was hurt.

Never mind that she'd never wanted to be in his presence again—the man had made her lose face the day before when she'd failed to recognize him, and she totally hated to have her pride stung. The doctor in her came to the fore, and she rushed to his side.

"Jaeden?"

He turned and blinked when he saw her, then he smiled. Her knees went weak from the sensual assault the sight stirred in her, but she forced herself to focus, and that's when she noticed the gash on his forehead and the dried blood that had crusted his eyebrow. Goodness, how long had he been injured?

"Let me look at you," she said softly as she cradled his face in her hands and went up on tiptoe to examine his head wound.

The bleeding seemed to have stopped there, but what about his leg?

"Shee," he said, awe heavy in his tone.

Great, he also wasn't making much sense. He could have a concussion after having hit his head.

She was already peering down at his hurt calf when he brought his hands up and covered hers where they still cradled his jaw.

The shock of heat and longing that raced through her entire body made her jerk. He pressed his palms into the backs of her hands and kept her touch in place, though.

"You're real," he said.

Zenobia had never been one for nonsense of any kind, and she shook herself out of his grip.

"Of course I'm real," she quipped.

"Crivvens, lass. Ye an ill-willie!"

She frowned. What had he just said?

"What?" she asked.

He shook his head. "Never mind."

His voice had sounded thicker, and it seemed to her he'd rolled his 'r' way too much.

"What happened to you?" she asked as she raked her gaze onto him from head to toe.

"Slipped, fell, hit my head. Now trying to get a signal so I can ring for help."

Yes, he might indeed have a concussion.

And if he did, there wasn't much she could do for him in this setting. His wounds, however, she could look after.

"Sit down. Let me take a look at this."

He beamed a bright smile onto her. "You're still not being nice to me."

She blinked and redirected her focus onto his head injury. No time or inclination here to play nice, thank you. They'd gotten off the wrong foot and so be it. She slung the backpack to the ground and unzipped it. After grabbing a packet of alcohol wipes, she pulled a soaked tissue from it and started to dab at his forehead.

To his credit, he didn't wince when the alcohol touched the cut. She'd stopped counting the times she'd lost respect for people just because they behaved like wusses when suffering from a tiny wound a kid would not fret about.

The area around the cut cleaned, she could see it was small and had stopped bleeding already. It would probably just need a butterfly stitch to bring the edges together again. His skin didn't feel hot, even though she encountered sweat, which wasn't surprising under the humid cover of the forest.

"Any nausea? Vomiting? Chills? Pain?"

He shook his head, and his eager dark brown gaze settled on her, making her squirm.

She deflected by looking at his calf. "Can you turn it around a bit?"

He complied, and she hissed in a breath when she saw the wound was still bleeding. Finding a clean compress in her bag, she then applied it to the gash, putting pressure on it. Silence fell between them. Actually, she should say words didn't flow, because his gaze was burning a hole in her, full of questions, puzzled.

After a while, she removed the compress, and upon seeing the bleeding had stopped, she proceeded to clean the wound and let it air dry before placing a sterile dressing on there.

Now, for the other question that needed to be answered. She glanced up and froze when she met his intense eyes.

A man with a concussion wouldn't look this sharp and composed.

Still, she had to ascertain.

"What's that smell?" he asked.

"What smell?"

He leaned forward then, dipped his head towards her neck. She shot her head back just as he took in a heady whiff of her skin.

"You. You smell like flowers and suntan lotion."

Zenobia could only gape at him. How had he picked up the faint whiff of the beauty oil she'd worn all over her body? Her bottle of Nuxe Huile Prodigieuse never left her because it moisturized as well as kept mosquitoes at bay in any tropical location—in other words, a godsend in Mauritius.

"Shee," he said again, now with a half-smile.

This was getting out of hand. Falling back onto medical protocol, she retrieved her cell phone and beamed the flashlight into his eyes. He snapped his lids closed, but not before she saw the tell-tale response of his irises.

"Follow my finger," she told him.

He did. Another good point.

"You're a doctor?" he asked.

"Yes." Any more than a clipped reply, she wouldn't be able to muster. This man's mere presence frazzled her nerves.

If there was one thing she absolutely hated, it was losing control. She'd worked hard to not lose herself to despair all through the years she'd spent under her stepmother's roof, and she'd become the mistress of her destiny the second she'd stepped over that threshold to never look back.

No man was going to make her lose her stand.

"What's your name?" he then asked.

She sent him a glare through her lashes.

"I'll call you Bunny then."

No mistaking the laughter in his tone right now. She also knew exactly why he'd chosen that name. Her massive front teeth had been the butt of jokes when she'd been in school, too. She'd developed a thick skin since then.

"Fine, K-Pop," she retorted.

At this, he guffawed.

She ignored him as she continued with her assessment. He'd smelled her body oil, so this meant no potential damage to the frontal lobe of the brain— a compromised sense of smell would've indicated that. And from the way he was smiling, the corners of his eyes crinkling with the emotion, he appeared fully able to move his facial muscles.

"Can you touch your nose first with the right index, then with the left?"

He could—motor coordination seemed good, too. It might not be a concussion, but he should get a CT scan nevertheless to make sure.

"You called me pretty yesterday, too," he ventured.

She frowned as she looked everywhere but at him. "I didn't call you pretty today."

"K-Pop. That's almost the same thing."

"It wasn't meant as a compliment," she quipped.

He chuckled. "I know. But in my defence, the red in my hair comes from my maw's DNA, not a chemical treatment."

Zenobia squinted at his hair. How had she not noticed that he did indeed have pronounced red highlights in the dark, swept-back mass? And drat, he seemed to have an answer for everything. She hated know-it-alls.

"You started it."

As the words rolled off her tongue, she wanted to slap her hands onto her mouth. How had she lost the little leverage she still had by going on the offensive like that?

"Me calling you Bunny? That's because you won't tell me your name." He paused, and his face clouded over, bringing a pang in her heart. "And you haven't been nice to me at all ever since we met."

When I have been, he didn't add.

She gulped as she admitted this and digested the blow. She'd thought he'd gotten on his high horse yesterday when he'd asked her if she didn't know who he was, but it had really been surprise talking, not conceit.

"Sorry," she bit out.

He stared at her for long seconds. "You don't mean it."

He held no inflection in his tone, and she recoiled as if burned by acid.

"We should get back," she mumbled.

"Do you know the way?"

She glanced up at the slope, now wrapped in low, grey clouds. No way could she take that path now. Also, with Jaeden's injury, he wouldn't be able to climb. The only solution would be to trek back the same way she'd come.

She stood and slung her zippered backpack over her shoulder.

"Over through there," she mentioned with a jerk of her head. "You up for it?"

CHAPTER THREE

He wasn't, but he wouldn't admit that to her. The really sensible thing would be to camp out here, especially now that she'd taken care of his wounds and also ascertained he didn't have a head injury, and wait for her to bring help back. But that could take hours, and he didn't have hours in him. Not in his condition.

"Lead the way," he told her.

A wince turned into a string of curses when he gripped the bark of the tree next to him and tried to pull himself up.

"We'll try to go over flat land, okay?" she said and handed him a bottle of water from her backpack.

He could only nod as he braced his spine and clamped his jaw before taking a few steps while hanging on to the foliage around him. The water felt like blessed relief down his throat as he gulped it down. She sure had come prepared.

"Be careful," she told him, easily slipping behind him.

"Guess you're a hiker then."

He heard a snort.

"What gave it away?"

He turned to smile at her. "Well, the bottomless bag that must also hold the remnants of Atlantis was a dead giveaway."

She chuckled. Damn, what he wouldn't do to get her to giggle again. Strangely enough, though she was giving him the cold shoulder, he actually enjoyed the interaction with her. It had been a while since he'd met a non-sycophant type. His people in Shetland usually treated him like their equal, and it had been weeks since he'd been back home. He'd missed the refreshing feeling of having someone not being in awe of him or fawning over him, especially a woman.

Yes, this one was playing very hard to get, but something told him it wasn't a wile or trick. No, this woman stayed on her guard. Why? He definitely intended to find out.

"So," he asked. "What happened to Atlantis?"

"How should I know?"

Some of the ice had thawed from her tone. Good. Progress.

"You mean it's not at the bottom of your bag?"

And there it was—that giggle.

"I just come prepared," she said.

"With such an elaborate first aid kit?"

"Where I work, you know never to step out without supplies because they're not available everywhere."

"And where is that?"

His step faltered, and he caught himself and shook his head. He had to make it out of this forest before he collapsed.

The silence stretched for so long, he thought she wouldn't answer.

"India," she finally said.

"You're a bit far from Kansas, Dorothy."

He smiled when she gave another soft giggle. This woman loved to laugh ... but she probably didn't have much chance to experience lightness in her life. Something in him just knew that.

"Kansas is not even India," she said, her tone free of any chill for the first time.

"Then where are you from?"

From her accent, he'd be tempted to say England, maybe even South London.

He slipped for real this time, and as dark spots blurred his vision, he heaved for breath. His heartbeat felt erratic, too. He was cutting it close.

"What's wrong?" she asked, and came around to stand in front of him.

She gasped as he lifted his face. Even he knew he must've paled by a few shades.

"You didn't seem to have a concussion," she said, her pitch getting higher.

Time to bite the bullet and admit his failing. "You wouldn't happen to have some candy or chocolate with you, aye?"

She raked her jade-green gaze over him. "Hypoglycaemia?"

He nodded. He didn't have diabetes or any of the rare conditions that could trigger low blood sugar so regularly, yet, no doctor had ever been able to explain this condition of his.

"You utter idiot! You came hiking without any sugar source on you?"

Damn, but anger resonated strongly in her voice when she let loose. She'd put a banshee to shame with that cadence.

"I carry a box of Tic-tac with me, but I lost it when I fell."

"I only have water bottles left," she said. "Goodness, we need to get you back up there ASAP."

She took her phone out, tried to find a signal. No luck.

"Do you remember what way you came? We might be able to find them ..."

She must've realised how pointless that question was—he would already have done that if he'd remembered.

She glanced around, and then her face lit up when she saw something. She went to a green bush and plucked a few of those red berries from there. When she got closer, he could see they looked more like guavas.

"Eat this," she told him.

Wait a second—she'd just told him she wasn't from here. How did she know this was even edible, let alone not poisonous?

"Go on."

"What is that?" he asked, caution ringing in his tone.

"I have no idea."

His turn to look at her, all flummoxed. "How do you know that's even safe?"

She rolled her eyes. "My friend was eating those just the other day. I've been seeing these fruits being sold from buckets on motorcycles at every street corner in Port-Louis."

"Still not sanitary," he mumbled. Yes, he was cutting his nose to spite his face, but he'd heard of stomach bugs on tropical islands. Not pretty.

"Okay, listen, K-Pop. I have just one bottle of water left, and I'm not wasting it washing fruit for germaphobe you."

"You're not the one facing gastro-whatever from ingesting that," he countered.

Her eyes sparkled with anger, and she pursed her lips before pushing one of the little red balls into her mouth.

"There. If we're to get sick, it's nothing a course of antibiotics can't cure. If you wish to lose consciousness, go into a coma, and then die as opposed to the possibility of a little stomach flu, be my guest."

When she put it like that ... Without a word, he reached for the berries in her hand and ate one. The tartness made him squint—he hadn't expected it to be so sharp. But on its coattails came a dose of natural sugar that did him good. He had a few more of the fruit, and when his body felt almost normal again, he glanced into her face.

"Thanks," he said.

"Better?"

He nodded.

"Let's go, then."

They trekked in silence, and she stayed slightly behind him. When a sudden boom resounded, she yelped, and he turned to her just as the skies opened and rain poured down on them.

She froze in her spot, bringing her hands up to cover her ears against the horrendous growls.

A thunderstorm. Here they were caught under trees. Not good.

As light burst across the darkened sky, he stilled and listened, counting the seconds. The next screech came thirty seconds later. He calculated it in his head—thirty divided by five; they might have just enough time.

Gently, he grabbed hold of her upper arms and blinked away the rain hitting his face as he looked at her. Her skin had blanched—she was scared.

"The storm is about six miles away," he told her. "Come on. We can make it."

She remained frozen, then shook her head.

"Trust me," he said, and those words seemed to spark something in her as she nodded.

Still, she didn't move. He'd have to take matters into his own hands. They'd been heading right all this time. He supposed they should continue that way.

As the thunder rumbled even louder, she let out a wail. Without thinking twice, Jaeden engulfed her in his arms, bending to drop a soft kiss onto her soaked hair.

"It's gonna be okay," he mumbled in her ear.

She burrowed into his side, and like this, slowly but surely, they moved out of the forest and reached the stairs they'd gone down to get to the bottom of the gorges.

He made her go up first. The steps were slippery— if she fell, he would catch her.

When they broke the last step and emerged onto the parking space, she stopped, then turned as if to make sure he'd also gotten up on the asphalt. He gave her a nod as he moved away from the staircase.

"Zayn!" a man called.

Jaeden looked up just in time to see her rush into the arms of a tall and good-looking bloke with amber-toned skin. He wrapped his big arms around her, and she buried herself against his chest. No one could deny that she had come home in that embrace.

She was taken … Of course she would be.

A flurry of activity erupted around him, and he paid the people just half an ear as he continued to stare at her. Pointless, for sure, but he could look, aye?

Then she broke away from the man and turned around, her gaze stopping on Jaeden. With a few steps, she had reached his side.

"I'm sorry," she said.

He could hear that she meant it this time. Still, he had to ask. "What for?"

"For being such an abject arse with you."

She smiled at him, and he couldn't resist smiling back just so she'd keep that beautiful grin on her pretty face.

"You're forgiven," he said. "Tell me your name."

Masochist of him, but he had to know what she was called. More than that, he needed to hear the sound, every nuance of it, as it rolled off her tongue and came from her mouth.

"Zenobia," she said, and turned to return to her man.

It was the most beautiful string of notes Jaeden had ever heard.

***

What had gotten into her to tell him her name? More than the apology—something she rarely copped to—why had she brought that level of familiarity between them now?

Throughout the return trip to Zach and Annabelle's house in her brother's car, the question had tormented her. Something had happened between her and Jaeden during their time trekking back in the forest. She'd been all set to keep her distance from him, both literally and figuratively, but then he'd taken her in his arms, and she'd felt it ... Tenderness, caring.

Jaeden Kang was by no means a jerk, which made him all the more dangerous.

As she sat on a chaise longue on the shaded deck beside the pool, Zenobia fiddled with the towel she'd dropped to her feet. The downpour meant her hair had been soaked through. While anyone else would be able to go for a blow-dry to ease the wetness off their locks, with her large braids and naturally curly hair, she couldn't do so.

So the towel had done the job of absorbing as much of the water as possible from her braids, and she basked in the ambient heat, letting them air dry now. She'd slipped into a pair of track shorts and a tank top of Annabelle's. All her stuff was at the hotel. Zach had refused to let her out of his sight for the afternoon, and she'd spent the past few hours sighing at his solicitous manner while Annabelle's three cats kept her company. Fifi, a tiny fluff ball with one leg missing, had decided her lap made for the best sleeping spot.

If her brother asked her if she was hungry one more time, she'd scream.

Blessed relief came in the form of Annabelle early in the evening.

"Jaeden's been released from the clinic. CT scan clear," she said as she waltzed in.

A sigh of relief escaped Zenobia. So he hadn't suffered a concussion, thank goodness. What would she have done if she'd misdiagnosed him?

Losing Jaeden would be, well, a tremendous loss … and it scared her stiff to wonder why she even thought that. He was just a pretty face, after all. Right?

Except, he also had a heart, and she was starting to see beyond the persona. The M&Ms in his entourage? A clever way to conceal his hypoglycaemia. Not at all the raving demands of a diva.

"He's been told to take it easy," Annabelle continued as she joined Zenobia on the deck. "Bon dié o, what happened to your hair?"

Zenobia gave her a rueful smile. "Braids meeting with water."

"Looks more like braids stripped of any moisture, if you ask me, no offense."

"None taken. That's exactly it." She sighed. "You would be a darling to tell Zach to lay off a little and let me go back to the hotel. I left the moisture spray in my vanity case there."

"I'll do you one even better. Come."

Intrigued, Zenobia got up, settled the sleeping cat on the chaise, and followed her to the en-suite bathroom of the main bedroom. She blipped the sight of her brother's clothing hanging in the adjoining walk-in wardrobe and his toiletries on the marble countertop with the double washbasins. While she loved to know that he had found his person, she didn't need to get deep into the details, no thank you. Because sometimes, looking too closely made one realise what one lacked …

She shrugged off the doldrums and gasped when Annabelle pulled open a wide drawer that could double as the super-stash at a major women's magazine's beauty department. Just about every kind of hair conditioner, mask, treatment, and spray was laid out in front of her.

With raised eyebrows and unable to utter a word, she looked at her brother's fiancée, who burst into laughter.

"Hello?" Annabelle said. "You think these are real? Two-thirds of them are fake."

She ruffled her thick mane for good measure.

Stunned, Zenobia could at the same time not deny that she had asked herself this same question upon first meeting the brunette. Such a small face and all that hair? It hadn't looked naturally natural, if that made any sense. And now, it did all make sense.

For the next hour, she indulged in BFF-type self-care and pampering with her future sister-in-law.

"And now, for the party," Annabelle said.

"What party?" Zenobia asked just as Zach said, "I don't think that's a good idea. She's had a tough day."

Annabelle rolled her eyes. "That's exactly why it's a great idea! She needs a break, Zach, and this will be just the thing."

"Where's that party at?" Zenobia asked.

"At the hotel. Continuing the event weekend."

Which meant Jaeden would be there …? "Is DJ Den MC-ing again? He shouldn't play after that injury today."

"Nah, I don't think he'll be there. Docs told him to rest up, remember? His manager told me he'd keep an eye on him."

In that case … She groaned. "I've got nothing to wear."

She didn't own party clothes in India, let alone having packed any for her travels here.

"I'm here, non?" Annabelle said, then shooed Zach out of the room. She went into the walk-in and came out with a hanger. "I have the perfect dress for you."

Ten minutes later, she was staring at her reflection in the standing mirror with a dubious frown. "Your idea of perfect and mine are nothing alike."

"Oh, come on, this dress was made for you," Annabelle sing-sang as she flitted around with a compact of shimmering bronzing powder in her hand and a fluffy brush dancing over Zenobia's features.

Well, if 'made for you' was synonymous with 'liquid gold poured all over you and leaving nothing to the imagination', then yes, this dress was indeed the perfect choice. While she and Annabelle wore the same size, Zenobia had curves. Annabelle, on the other hand, looked like she should belong on a TV show like The Biggest Loser as one of those super-ripped trainers. Clothes tended to drape on her, unlike the brunette on whom they hung like on models walking the runway. The dress, which should be knee-length on the other woman, flirted with her ankles.

"Oh, live a little, will you? It's the eve of Valentine's Day. It's a magical time."

She had to admit, however, that when Annabelle had finished with her, she literally glowed from head to toe.

What was the worst that could happen tonight? She'd come here to see her brother, sure, but she'd also come to have some fun. When she went back to India, Dr. Crenshaw would soon enough drop the whole derelict mess they called a hospital on her shoulders. She should enjoy herself while she could.

Plus, Jaeden wasn't supposed to be there. She didn't know how she would face him again. From what she'd gathered, he would be leaving for Dubai and from there on to Australia on Monday. She just had to stay off his radar for the next two days, and she'd be fine.

For her own sake, really. Jaeden Kang shook and stirred things in her, and she wasn't a martini who ended up better when either shaken or stirred. Quite the opposite, in fact.

She ignored Zach's raised eyebrow when she emerged from the room, and a silent glare on her part pre-empted the 'Are you gonna wear that?' protective big brothers like hers were notorious for. With her phone and key card in a small gold pouch Annabelle had attached to her wrist, she got into the car with them and left for the party.

And a few hours later, she had to admit she was having the time of her life. Mauritians sure knew how to enjoy themselves. The event tonight was very informal, music and drinks flowing freely as people mingled and danced. Someone, probably the lead dancer from the hotel's entertainment troupe, had gotten onto the stage next to the DJ booth and directed the crowd into the choreography of the iconic songs being played. They'd done the Macarena, Gangnam Style, and right now, had the right knee lifted and their clenched hands pumping out to the catchy rhythm of Anuel AA's China.

Midnight must have come and gone already, but Zenobia didn't care. She was having too much fun.

Something caught her attention as she moved, and she froze on the dance floor. Was that Jaeden in the DJ booth? He seemed to be whispering something in the ear of the spiky-haired woman working the playlist tonight, and when she turned and gave him a radiant smile, Zenobia suddenly found herself fuming and wanting to wipe that smirk off her pretty face.

Miffed by the unexpected feeling that had just felled her—had it been jealousy?—she turned around and tried to pick up the rhythm again. No way she'd let anyone see what had just flared through her. The thought of Jaeden with someone else— No! She was not going there.

Just then, the pitch of the music changed, and she could make out the telltale guitar notes opening of Despacito. Zach turned and gave her a wink before he swept Annabelle into his arms and started swaying to the song with her. Any more sensuality and they could just have sex there, why not? But still, she smiled, albeit wistfully, as she watched her brother so happy with the woman he loved and who appeared to love him just as much.

If only she could have that, too, one day ... If someone like Zach who had sworn off love had found it, maybe ...

She shook her head. Wishful thinking. She didn't 'do' love, full stop. Suited her just fine.

This was a couple's song—she should get off the dance floor and go get a drink.

Her ear attuned to the beat, she frowned. Anyone must know the pitch and rhythm of this track that had been a worldwide smash hit. She didn't recall the dip towards the chorus happening so quickly at the start.

And then as the word rang—'Des-paaa ...'— someone grabbed her hand and pulled on it, twirling her back towards them. She'd been dancing with random strangers all night, so she just sighed, about to make her excuses. But then, strong palms settled on her either side of her rib cage, and—at '... cito'—those hands pulled her forward, her stomach slamming against someone's torso, as the couples in the original music video did during their dance.

Who ...? She should look at him before she kneed that guy in his balls, right?

Her breath got knocked out of her when she collided with this male figure, but even more so as she glanced up, and up, and up ... into Jaeden Kang's serious face and intense eyes.

Right then, she could do nothing except let out a puff of air as her body relaxed and he smoothly flowed into the rhythm, taking her along for the ride. His hands felt so right on her, the hard planes of his body fitting perfectly against her curves.

All through the song, the severity never left his face, drying her throat all the more. Her heart jumped with every brush of their bodies, every time he twirled her around before effortlessly pulling her back against him as if he were a magnet calling to her and she, made entirely of iron fillings. They flowed into one another. So perfectly. So naturally.

And when he pulled her even closer with a forearm that felt like a tight band of steel around her back, Zenobia knew to no longer fight the inevitable. It had been just a little over twenty-four hours since they'd met, but this had been a long time coming. Her soul knew it with utmost certainty, and so did his—she could read it in the passion that darkened his eyes and hardened every inch of his delectable body.

As the song eased into the beats and notes of Señorita, she leaned into him and went on tiptoe even in her three-inch sandals.

"Take me to your room," she uttered.

He blinked slowly. "You're sure? There's no turning back if we do …"

"I'm only going forward, not back," she said, taking his hand to subtly tug on it and pull him out of the venue, outside onto the beach.

To her relief, he complied.

They walked in silence after she'd ditched her shoes, slinging them from her hand, the voices of Shawn Mendes and Camila Cabello carrying them along, echoing so much of what was going on inside Zenobia. She couldn't fight this, because she didn't want to. If only she didn't need him … But she did. That's what she had fathomed all these hours ago on the parking lot of the national park as she'd gone up to him and had ended up telling him her name. She really should be running, but, to where? Everything would lead her back to this man.

She turned and gazed up at his face illuminated by the sapphire glow of the moonlight. Even in a short-sleeved shirt with a tie loosely knotted around the open neck of his collar and cargo shorts on, he should look like a fashion disaster, yet he reminded her of a Japanese anime prince, daintily beautiful but hiding hard strength nevertheless under all that gorgeousness.

At that moment, he peered down at her. Everything in her froze, but it was also the most ravishing feeling as all her cells seemed to respond to the pull of attraction he held over her.

He stopped. They now stood in front of a stand-alone villa opening directly onto the beach. He stared at her, as if unwilling to break the spell with a sound. But then, he did speak, uttering her name. She'd always known it sounded unusual, but rolling off his tongue, it struck her as the most crystalline sound ever. If she wasn't kidding herself, she would say she'd heard a reverent tone of worship in those three syllables.

Dare she find out if that were true?

Instinct bade her to go on the tip of her toes and seek her answer. So she did just that. Inch by painful inch, she let her body touch his, from her knees to her thighs to her belly, her breasts, until finally, her lips pressed against his and he opened up to her.

He tasted of something rich and flavoursome, like a Blanco tequila that had been sipped conscientiously after being given time to open properly in its glass. It felt like a drug as much as an aphrodisiac, and when his hands found their way onto her ribcage again, something in her knew she could give herself to this man, and she would be the safest she'd ever been in her whole life.

Zenobia let him take over the kiss, and when she plastered herself to him, he broke off, panting, and took her hand to lead her to the other side of the villa, where he opened the front door.

Animalistic lust took over once they got inside. Lips met, mouths clashed, tongues danced duets as hands dipped into hair and legs carried them to the main bedroom. They exchanged no words—they didn't have to, because they were talking a language as old as time and which they both knew fluently.

Gasps left her mouth as Jaeden kissed her jaw, the column of her neck, used his lips to actually undress her, the fragile gold fabric falling away before his wet tongue lapped at every inch of skin he uncovered. Not to be left behind, she quickly ripped the tie off him and tore his shirt open.

"Shee," he said with a laugh.

She should ask him what that meant, but the words died on her tongue as he pushed her onto the bed and grabbed the tie, wrapping it once around her wrists which he'd clasped together.

He paused then, looking into her eyes, asking if that was okay.

Fine by her. That's how she loved it—how did he know?

To show her compliance, she arched her back and stretched herself out on the king-sized bed, extending her arms as far as they'd comfortably go and crossing her wrists one over the other so he could tie them with the strip of silk.

He trailed the tips of his fingers along the sensitive inner skin of her arms when he'd finished the knot, causing shivers to course through her and yearning to build even more in her belly. Her breasts grew heavy, the pointed nipples almost hurting. Then he stood and raked his hungry gaze slowly over her from head to toe, making her burn under the intense, lascivious scrutiny. Without removing his eyes from her, he undid the rest of his clothing and stood proudly naked in front of her at the foot of the bed.

Her breath hitched in her lungs at the mouth-watering picture he presented. Long, sinuous muscle well-honed by exercise, not an ounce of fat, yet his body also looked lived-in, not that of a Ken doll come to life.

When he slowly climbed onto the mattress, a moan tore out of her, its intensity increasing ten-fold as he dipped forward and started feasting on her. She wanted to squirm under the intense pleasure, but he'd tied her up, and she'd agreed to play the part. So she contained her ecstasy, which in turn served to ratchet up the sensations even more.

Every inch of her skin, he worshipped. He would start at her core, bring her to the brink of a climax, then painstakingly go down her legs, before returning to tease her the same way again, then moving up her abdomen, to her breasts, to her mouth where she tasted herself on his lips.

She couldn't take this anymore, but the greatest pleasure came from delayed gratification. She knew that, and so did he. Jaeden was an ardent and unselfish lover, knowing how to ramp up her expectations.

She thought the ultimate bliss would come when he melted into the vee of her opened legs, and the tip of his protected cock touched the slickened wetness of her opening. He pushed slightly forward, and she hitched in a breath ... only for him to pull out, grip her hips, and flip her over onto her front before he plunged into her sheath from behind, eliciting a gasp of surprise turned pleasure that quickly wrung the most intense orgasm of her life from her very core.

On and on, she crested and fell, crested and fell, while he took her over and over and finally found his own release, screamed her name, and then fell on top of her, his forearms trying to brace himself at her sides so he wouldn't crush her.

Spent, she could just lie there. She should be thinking of leaving, but she couldn't. Not after this kind of earth-shattering rapture.

In a state of half-bliss, half-sleep, she felt him reach up and gently unwind the tie from around her wrists.

"Stay," he whispered in her ear.

She could only nod and burrow into the bed, then into him as he wrapped his big body around her back and spooned with her.

She should be making her excuses and leaving, thinking of the silk scarf she should wrap her braids in if she didn't want disaster come morning. But as exhaustion and slumber caught up with her, the only thing she could think of was how it would sound if he'd said 'Zayn' instead of 'Zenobia' when he came.

CHAPTER FOUR

Jaeden couldn't quite believe it when he opened his eyes and found her still in his arms.

Last night had been … He didn't have words for it. A cornucopia of sounds to express joy and enlightenment, yes—he could string that together. Words, however, eluded him.

He had known he wanted her from the moment he'd seen her. No denying that. But wanting felt pale and insignificant in light of what he'd experienced with her when they'd made love. So this must be the once-in-a-lifetime kind of experience all bards and poets and artists raved about.

He'd thought her off-limits to him after seeing her in the parking lot the previous day. Then, at the party, he'd seen the guy she'd been with dancing with Annabelle in a sexy way that proclaimed to the world they were a couple and probably burning the sheets in the privacy of their lives. That's when he'd gone into the DJ's booth and had asked her to play 'Despacito,' asking her to bring the chorus forward by a few beats, enough time for him to find Zenobia on the floor and sweep her into the choreography.

He'd played his all on that dance, taking the risk she might've slapped him in the face or kneed him in the bollocks when he'd so possessively made his claim on her. He wasn't a macho man, but his Norse heritage had come forward when he'd seen her. Norsemen took because they set their sights on strong women who would strike back if they thought the bloke had crossed a line; they risked themselves and their balls.

But she'd gone along with it, had flowed into him, merging the heat of her sinful body with his … and they'd made magic together.

For how much longer, he didn't know, but he had her now, and he wouldn't relinquish her.

She stirred in her sleep, then hummed a sound from deep in her throat and arched her back to stretch herself out. The sheet fell off her chest, exposing the gorgeous, full globes of her brown breasts with their dusky pink tips.

When she opened her eyes, he braced himself to see regret or panic in them. A punch landed in his gut as he fell into those green irises which, right now, reminded him of the Mirrie Dancers—what they called the Northern Lights in Shetland.

She was magical, all right. A sith.

She frowned a little, then smiled at him. "What does that mean?"

"What?" he asked.

"Shee. You've said that quite a few times now."

He must've said the word aloud right now without realizing it. "It means faery in the North."

"You're from the North?"

He liked how she hadn't bolted from the bed, or even made any effort to cover up. He appreciated this about her—how she had no pretence. What you saw was what you got. He missed that kind of refreshing honesty in his life.

"So?" she asked with a raised brow.

She'd asked him a question. "Aye. Shetland."

"Which is?"

"A group of islands to the north of Scotland."

"But part of Britain."

"Since the fifteenth or sixteenth century, part of Scotland."

"Oh."

She still hadn't moved. He was loving this pillow talk with her.

"You reckon I don't even know your full name," he said.

She smiled, which wrapped a hand around his entrails and squeezed hard.

"Zenobia Hashemi."

"And you're from?"

She made him sweat for long seconds when he thought she wouldn't answer him.

"Tanzania," she finally said.

And boarding or private school would explain the clipped British accent. Her family must be loaded. Unlike his, though he'd made a fortune and had set up both his parents in luxury. He wasn't ashamed of his origins, had never been, but some people really had had it better than him in life. These people also tended to throw that in the face of anyone they considered beneath them.

He should get over this insecurity that could come out of nowhere to plague him at times. Zenobia had proven she wasn't a snob.

Her face grew dark, and she clasped the sheet to her chest. "What?"

She must've seen the expression of his thoughts flitter on his face.

"I was just wondering how in Tanzania you turned out looking like you did."

Let's just say that made sense.

Well played, Kang!

"It's a very diverse country, you know."

"I do, which is what got me thinking."

Great. Keep at it. Seriously?

Then she giggled. That amazing sound he had fallen in love with.

A smile settled on her face, but something struck him right then. Zenobia Hashemi had a broken smile.

He'd actually seen that in the parking lot of the national park the previous day, but he hadn't been able to put his finger on it until now.

Everything in him surged ahead, wanting to do whatever he could to make her happy, to make her smile genuine. Why him, he asked himself? Then again, why not him?

"My father is an Ismaili Muslim. My mother was Somali. Mix the two, and you get brown kids like my brother and me."

Right—the other guy was her sibling.

Something felt off in what she'd said. "Was?"

Her features tightened for a second before she answered. "She passed away when we were little."

"I'm sorry." A platitude, indeed, but also true.

"Got over it," she said as she forced her face to brighten up again.

Have you?

"What about you?" Turning onto her side, she pressed her cheek into her palm.

Less loaded territory—he should take the cue.

"My father is Korean, lives in Glasgow now. My maw's family is originally from Norway, and she still lives in Shetland."

"Hmm, so it makes sense now," she said, then frowned slightly as she looked around.

He turned onto his side to face her. "What makes sense?"

"That you ask for Arctic temps and AC everywhere. Though it doesn't feel Arctic here right now. How come?"

He winced. "That. A fallacy concocted by my manager."

"Like the M&Ms because you need sugar every so often."

She'd figured him out. He nodded.

"Don't you need breakfast or at least some orange juice or something now?"

He chuckled. "Yes, Doc. But I'm still feeling okay right now and will get something soon."

She quirked an eyebrow at him.

"Promise," he said. "Did you always want to be a doctor?"

She shrugged. "I had an affinity for it."

A lot she wasn't telling him in that answer, but he'd let it pass.

"Did you always want to be a DJ?"

"I'm a music producer, actually."

"And what does a music producer do, actually?"

"Make music."

"Right."

Suddenly, an idea hit home, and it seemed perfect. "Come with me today. I'll show you."

She squinted and stared at him as if weighing her reply.

"Okay," she finally said.

He released the breath he hadn't known he'd been holding. "Meet me at Reception in one hour."

And until he found her again, standing in the flowered colonnade that made up the entrance into the hotel's Reception lobby, his heart had beat with an erratic rhythm not unlike what he felt when his blood sugar dropped dangerously low.

She'd changed into a strappy sundress that bared her rounded shoulders and exposed her long arms and limbs to their best light. The braids that usually framed her face had been lifted into a sort of top knot at the back of her skull, the rest of them flowing down her spine to flirt with the curved small of her back. Dainty flat sandals encased her feet, a white straw beach bag hanging from her hand.

She smiled when she saw him, but he couldn't help but feel that she was slipping away somewhat.

And what did that matter? Neither of them did long-term, as far as he'd grasped.

He shook the unnerving feeling away and started towards her. He'd sent Fergus out on a fool's errand so he'd have the rest of the day free with Zenobia.

"Where are we off to?" she asked when he reached out and slung an arm around her back.

"It's a surprise."

She groaned.

"Don't like surprises?" he asked with a chuckle.

"No."

"Trust me on that," he said with a wink as they stopped by a car and he opened the back door so she could get in, then he followed. He nodded at the driver who already knew their destination, and off they went.

Comfortable silence lulled between them. He liked that she didn't feel she had to babble away to fill the quiet. This woman knew what she wanted, aye. Yesterday, she'd wanted him. Could he make that last?

He frowned as the thought crossed his mind. Where had that come from? Tomorrow, he would be leaving this island, and at some point, she'd go back to India where she worked. They were ships meeting in a transient port.

His mother always told him that's how she and his father had started out, too ... He clamped his jaw. That might be true enough, and they'd stayed together for over a decade and had him somewhere along that timeline, but it hadn't lasted, in the end. That's what mattered.

They'd arrived at a massive iron gate which opened as soon as the car drew up to it. Jaeden sat up straighter and flung the door open before the engine had even been killed. The driver opened the door for Zenobia, and she got out and looked at the structure before them, which resembled a pile of big rectangular blocks stashed by a toddler with no idea of harmony.

He waited for her to join him, then started up the stairs to the front door, which swung open to let out a string-thin White bloke with a shaved head and more piercings than features on his face.

He and Guillaume exchanged a complicated hand choreography as a greeting, then he introduced their host to Zenobia.

"It's all yours, man," Guillaume said, giving him a pat on the back. "Stunner, by the way, your gal," he added in a murmur like a conspirator.

Zenobia however blushed, and the rush of soft colour to her cheeks made him smile. She looked even more beautiful like that.

"Come on, let's go in," he told her.

He waved for her to precede him, then once inside, oriented himself from the signage on the doors. As much as he would love to just open a random panel and tug her into the room to have his wicked way with her again, he did reckon that the drums room, for example, would not make a very good setting for a heated quickie.

He'd bide his time. They still had today.

Locating the door to the studio, he pushed it and slipped inside the dim, sound-proof interior. He closed the door behind her, and an afterthought made him lock it. Fergus might find out where he was, and his manager wouldn't be averse to barging in with no respect for what Jaeden could be doing inside. Zenobia deserved better than that.

"So this is your workplace," she said after taking a turn around and dropping her bag on the floor near the couch.

"Pretty much, aye."

She smiled at him, looking like a wee lassie in a sweets shop. The excitement positively sparkled from her green eyes. "Show me."

He breathed in, relishing how it felt to be in his element again. While he loved mixing music at events and festivals, he found his true calling inside a studio with a laptop and other gear scattered around. At first glance, he could already see Guillaume had gone all out with the setting and layout. The equipment was some of the best. His gaze landed on the Prophet 6 synthesizer by Dave Smith, and he smiled. To the untrained eye, this looked like a musical keyboard with a wide span of dials and buttons. Oh, the magic he could create with that.

Still, he'd promised Guillaume he'd put the whole studio to the test, and that was where Zenobia came in.

"Sing for me," he told her.

She appeared baffled, then a burst of laughter rippled from her throat. "Are you out of your mind?"

He chuckled, too. "Not at all. That's the recording booth. Get in there, and I'll show you what I do."

"I sing like the worst ever Idol audition you've ever heard."

"Trust me on that," he said with a wink.

She eyed him for long seconds. "You're not gonna show me if I don't get in there, right?"

He gave her another wink. She shrugged and made for the door, then got into the booth.

"Do I put on those headphones?"

"No need. You're just going to talk to me, and I'll record that."

She seemed surprised. "That's it?"

He nodded, closed the door, and went to the console. He could clearly see her across the wide glass pane, just as she could see him.

He got to work and started a dialogue with her, adjusting the gains so her voice would ring clearer, then started recording. They spoke of everything and nothing, and he teased her, hitting pay dirt when she giggled. The very sound he'd come here looking for. He played it back, and it rang in his ear, crystal-clear from the headphone.

At this, he motioned for her to come out. She exited the sound booth, but he was already busy isolating her voice on the track and mixing it to smooth it out and run some other effects through it before mastering it and adding further details.

He didn't know for how long he remained in his bubble like this until he felt a soft hand on his shoulder and heard Zenobia calling him.

He blinked out of his zone and stared at her, for the first few seconds wondering where he was and what they were doing there.

"Hey," she said with a smile.

"Hi," he replied, still a bit discombobulated.

"Eat," she said, pushing an energy bar into his hand.

"I don't—" The world swirled around him, and he reeled.

"It's been two hours, Jaeden. You have to get your blood sugar up."

He nodded and accepted the bar, taking a bite and swallowing without really tasting what he'd eaten. The shakes fluttered out soon after.

"I hope there's someone to look after you whenever you're in the studio," she said.

He nodded. "Aye. Cassie."

Did he imagine this, or had her face darkened upon hearing that name?

"She's my best mate Paul's wife. We all grew up together in Shetland."

"Okay. Good."

Something kept puzzling him, and he blurted it out. "You've been watching me for two hours?"

She giggled, which made his knees go weak. How he loved that sound, and now, he'd have it for all eternity, on a recording.

"It was fun listening to what you were doing. I didn't know you could do all that with just one sound as the base."

He grinned. "That's not everything. Wait 'til you hear— Ow!"

"What? What's wrong?"

He grimaced and shrugged his body out of the chair.

"These seats are awful. Will have to tell Guillaume. Someone needs to be able to sit in there for an all-nighter and be comfortable. Let's move to the couch," he said, lifting the slim laptop in the process.

They settled on the plush, comfortable sofa, and he ran her voice through the software, showing her what it sounded like with auto-tune correcting the pitch, for example.

He had no clue how much time passed, and then, he looked up, catching her eyes which once again reminded him of Mirrie Dancers.

"Damn, you're gorgeous," he said in a whisper.

She giggled. "You're not so bad-looking yourself."

All lightness left him then and there; it felt like a life-altering moment all of a sudden.

"I'm not joking, Zenobia."

She stared at him with her lips slightly parted, her eyes big and inquisitive. Then she licked those lips before biting the fuller lower one.

"Zayn," she said. "People close to me call me Zayn."

"Zayn," he repeated, his voice an awed hush.

Her brother had called her by that moniker when she'd rushed into his arms. It was a special name, a favour, which she'd now bestowed on him.

Jaeden couldn't help himself. He leaned in and claimed her soft lips with his, drinking from this heated kiss that fired him up. Poison, he thought when he broke free and peered into her jade eyes. She was poison in his blood.

And damn, did that feel great … It would be his death, sure, but the rush before it killed …

He only had the presence of mind to place the laptop on the side table before he dived in for seconds, helping himself to what she gave freely as she lay back and opened her arms to welcome him in her embrace.

The sundress ended up in a crumpled mass somewhere under their writhing bodies, his clothes having landed on the floor.

Sometime during his worship of her breasts, a thought struck him. He'd asked her that before in the recording booth, but she hadn't answered back then.

He lifted himself up on one arm to gaze at her under him on the sofa. "I like you, you know."

Do you like me, too?

He didn't say it, though, and he imagined, for a split-second, that she'd read the question in his eyes.

What did it matter if she liked him, though? They would be going their separate ways soon enough.

The idea filled him with dread for a fraction of a moment, and she broke the paralyzing feeling when she spoke.

"We're friends, Jaeden."

And just like that, her words rang like a dismissal to him. She was keeping her wits about her; he should be doing the same. But he couldn't.

He slipped down her body until the soft thatch of curls covering her mound feathered the tip of his nose. "Tell me, do friends know the way you taste?"

Then he plunged in, not waiting for her response, unable to wait for it. Her back arched, and he took the opportunity to delve deeper into her, to bring her to the brink. His lips on her clit, he searched for his shorts at the foot of the couch with his free hand. Finding it, he tore himself away just long enough to extract a condom and roll it on his length before he went into her willing body, his soul falling into the bottomless abyss of her green irises.

They made love like this, never losing eye contact even as they soared and crested the wave together this time. She sang his name, just as he crooned hers. "Zayn ..."

Spent, he let his body drop onto hers, rolling them both onto their side so he wouldn't crush her.

The question kept ringing in his head. With his mouth against her ear, he asked, "Do they?"

She didn't answer, and this drove him as mad as it made him fathom that there wouldn't be more between them.

"You're poison running through my veins ..." he muttered.

Long moments later, she stirred. "So are you to me."

That whisper was the last thing he heard from her before she got up and exited his life.

CHAPTER FIVE

Five weeks later

Damn it! Why wasn't anything working?

Jaeden was almost tempted to tear through the equipment in his home studio on the Shetland Mainland as the latest sound—probably the hundredth he'd attempted in the recent weeks— screeched into a horrendous riff somewhere along the line.

Had he lost his touch? Anytime he sat down to start a vibe, the notes would flow for a few seconds, then spiral into gibberish. At first, he'd blamed it on exhaustion—the tour in Australia had been demanding, and the climate and temperature shock from the Gold Coast in summer to Shetland in winter hadn't helped matters.

But damn it. It had been two weeks since he'd sat down in this studio to try and work a new sound. So far, nothing.

Upon hearing the little voice that told him that wasn't true, he closed his eyes tight and pinched the bridge of his nose. He had, indeed, been working on something. Just not what he wanted to focus on.

Reluctantly, his mind went back to the long hours he'd spent on Splice, the equivalent of iTunes for music producers, looking for sound bites and other feels that would bring to mind the birds in the Mauritian forest, the swish of the lagoon ... and drums and other instrumentals from the Serengeti located in Tanzania. Over it all, he'd worked in little bits of voice that had been haunting him ever since Valentine's Day.

He had been fine initially. She'd left—so what? It was never meant to be anything more than a fling between them. When he'd pushed just a little, she'd brought him back in line.

He clenched his jaw as the thought hit. She hadn't felt much more than lust for him. Which should've been perfect; that's how the best relationships worked, in his opinion. Both people getting in knowing exactly what they wanted and how to get it.

But had he really known what he wanted? Not sure. Because he'd felt things with her, for her ... Things he couldn't explain or reason through. And there lay the clincher. The sense he'd somehow been blindsided by an unknown force.

He'd returned to the hotel that day feeling utterly bereft. Other than going through Annabelle, he'd had no idea how to contact Zenobia. The woman didn't even have a social media presence, as far as he'd gathered. He'd found references to her illustrious family in the media, though, her father being a rich industrialist in Tanzania.

And maybe that was for the best. He should forget her, he'd told himself over and over that day. Once he'd left Mauritius, he had. Australia had been hectic and boisterous and demanding and utterly exhausting—exactly what he'd needed. But back in Shetland with nothing on his agenda for the foreseeable future, the demons had slowly started slithering out, fuelled by the poison—the potent, beautiful poison—she had infused in his system.

That's how he'd found himself in the studio mixing and mastering the sound of her voice. Her giggle had almost become a lifeline before he'd forced himself to put that track aside and focus on something else … which had turned into nothing else, however.

Damn it! What was he supposed to do now?

As the anger bubbled inside him, he took a deep breath and forced himself out of his seat and exited the studio. On the outskirts of Lerwick, the Shetland capital, it would take him just a few minutes' walk from his house to some cliffside where the sound of the waves crashing against the rocks would silence all the turmoil brewing inside his mind.

He should do that—those walks had become a daily feature ever since he'd come back. Something seemed to be working at him, eating at him, and he had no idea what. It had felt like inspiration ready to burst out of him, yet his time in the studio had proven that to be a moot point. So the tempest gathered inside him and would explode soon if he didn't find an outlet for it. If only he bloody knew what that feeling inside wanted from him!

A cold wind slapped his face when he stepped out. Darkness was already falling despite it being sometime in the afternoon. He really shouldn't venture out there all alone. Still, his other option would be to go back in, to a studio that felt increasingly claustrophobic, or head next door to his mates Paul and Cassie's place.

He grimaced. Going there would feel like intruding. Cassie had recently found out she was pregnant, and Paul was doting on his wife. All that domestic bliss tended to make Jaeden sick, although he tried not to delve too deep into the real beef he had with this image. Why did Paul get to be so happy? Petty of him to think that way, so he refused to go there both literally and figuratively.

However, as he zipped his anorak and set out towards the cliff, the decision fell out of his hands. Paul was rushing his way.

"Jae, you have to come see this," his friend said as soon as he'd caught up.

Jaeden didn't like the ring of helplessness in the tone. "Everything all right? Cassie?"

Damn, he loved those two like the siblings he'd never had, having known them since kindergarten.

"No, not Cassie. You better sit down for this."

Paul grabbed his shoulder and pushed him towards his own house. Jaeden's breath grew stilted just as his heartbeat went erratic. Nothing good could come from this—he could feel it in his bones, in the chill that had nothing to do with the weather inserting itself in him.

Inside the cosy dwelling, he ditched his jacket and moved to the couch where Cassie sat with a worried expression on her pretty face.

"What's wrong?" he asked.

Paul swiped his phone and handed it over. Music started playing, and everything inside Jaeden plunged to his knees as he recognized the cords and notes. Dread wrapped itself around in his chest, and he looked up at his best friend.

"It wasn't me," Paul said softly.

"Of course it wasn't you. That vibe is only half-finished."

Paul was even more of a perfectionist than Jaeden himself—the reason they worked so well together. Never would the best pro-mixing engineer in the world have let such a half-baked track out. The auto-tune in some parts made the female voice sound like a bad rip-off of The Weeknd.

Then it all clicked. Only one person could've done this.

"Fergus," he mumbled.

"Aye," Paul replied.

"Tell him to come down here." They had a score to settle now. What had the tube been thinking? It wouldn't be pretty. He turned to Cassie. "It could get nasty, mo ghràdh. I'll take it next door."

"Yer bum's oot the windae, ye fuckin' bampot!" she threw out at him, along with a cushion.

He chuckled, having expected no less than she'd tell him he was an unhinged tit talking rubbish. So be it, then. He'd stay.

Paul made the call, then went to the kitchen to turn on the kettle. Armed with a mug of tea each, they waited. He could feel his friends brimmed with questions, yet they kept themselves in check.

Fergus finally flounced in, looking nonplussed.

None of them greeted him, Jaeden instead turning on the music, letting it play for a few seconds, then switching it off. "What the fuck, Fergus?"

To his credit, the bloke, who looked like the result of a hamster having a baby with a pelican, maintained a poker face.

"I did ye a favour," the man finally said.

Jaeden frowned. "How do you work that one out?"

"Ach, come on. Yer got a face lit like a melted welly since Australia."

He looked miserable—good enough reason to leak his raw music behind his back?

"Listen, Jae," Fergus continued. "Yer last hit was a fuckin' full year ago! Yer fans need something to bite before they forget ye."

He shook his head. Now he got it. Fans meant downloads and sales and ultimately, money. All his manager was concerned about.

He should've seen this coming. Yet, loyalty counted for something. Fergus had been shaping him into something he wasn't in the public eye, but as long as he'd been allowed to make his music, he'd been okay. Even that had been sullied now. Because this track was personal, being all about Zenobia.

"You're fired," he told his manager.

Fergus grew red and started spluttering. Paul didn't wait for more shenanigans before grabbing the man by the shoulders and hefting him out of the house. A few seconds later, they heard the sound of a slamming car door and a vehicle tearing out in a hiss of gravel.

When he came back in, he exchanged a nod with his wife, who turned to Jaeden.

"This is blowing up on social media, Jae."

He nodded, having expected as much. "I'll need to change the passwords."

"On it," Cassie said.

She'd been his social media handler before Fergus had brought in some pimply-faced tit from Scalloway.

She worked on for a little while, then put the phone down. "I've let your contacts know that Fergus is no longer your manager and that all communication is to come through me for the foreseeable future. It's not damage control, but you'll need to do something about this, Jae."

He knew that. Where to start, though?

"Jae, who is she?" Paul asked, breaking the silence.

He lifted his head. No point pretending. So he told them all about Zenobia, how they'd met, how they'd parted. Somewhere along his discourse, he smiled as a notion came to him. People often said how they'd fallen in love at first sight. While he … He'd fallen in love at first sound with her giggle.

This made him sit up straighter. He looked at his friends.

"Does that mean …?"

"That ye love her? Aye, Jae. I think it does," Cassie said softly.

His heart started hammering. He'd lost her, though, for good.

He ran a hand over his face in despair and weariness. "What do I do now?"

"I have an idea," Cassie said.

***

"Dr. Hashemi! If it wouldn't be imposing on your time to take a look at the patient in Room Four."

Zenobia winced and nodded towards Dr. Crenshaw before hightailing it to the room in question. Great, another tourist who'd gone gallivanting around and had thus torn their ankle on a piece of rusty metal hidden in the tall grass of the fields at the edge of this coastal village.

The sight of the hurt leg brought to mind another injury she'd tended to, and she forced herself to blip that image out. Because thinking of Jaeden would only make her hurt.

Whenever she closed her eyes, she remembered how he'd looked on that couch in that studio as she'd slithered from underneath his solid, warm body to then gather her clothes, put them on, and leave, never glancing back.

It hadn't driven home yet until just before that moment that she had fallen in love with him. The knowledge hadn't scared her; it had simply made sadness permeate every cell of her being. She'd never 'done' love because she had no idea what it meant to love. The little Zach had given her growing up, bless him, had been but a few drops into the cup of her heart. The rest had remained dreadfully empty her whole life.

So how would she be able to give when she had nothing to give? Jaeden had accused her of being poison running through his veins. What did poison do except destroy? She should know, considering how he'd turned into the same in her blood, irreversibly altering her life. Because now she knew … She couldn't go back. Malin, her friend with benefits, had taken just one look at her upon her return and then come close to drop a chaste kiss on her forehead.

"It hurts, doesn't it?" he'd asked.

She'd simply nodded. Unrequited love was indeed a bitch.

She'd wondered how she would cope, if life at the hospital would be enough. As luck would have it, family drama had landed right on her doorstep to keep her more than occupied in the weeks that followed her return from Mauritius. Rayan, their half-sibling, had come knocking on her door one night. On a visit in neighbouring Pakistan with their father and his mother to secure an alliance for him there, he had eloped with a young woman—not his betrothed—and the couple had come to her for help.

Pandemonium would've been putting it mildly— she'd called Zach in a state of panic, and he'd taken the next flight to India to sort this mess out. In the end, their little brother and his girlfriend both being Muslims, Zach had been able to arrange a religious wedding for them, the families then having no choice but to accept their union.

While she'd lived in that Bollywood drama, Jaeden and any thought of him had been blissfully far from her considerations. Not anymore, though. Now that she had the headspace to think … it got dismal in there at times. Things weren't looking dire per se, but more lacklustre. And that was driving her slowly insane. She was thirty-three, for Heaven's sake, with her whole life ahead of her. Would she be turning into some sort of Mother Teresa figure here, caring for the needy and downtrodden on the Indian subcontinent?

A beep came from her cell phone—a message from Annabelle. The woman had been apprising her of the latest news in the saga they'd all reluctantly gotten embroiled in. This latest text would be of the same vein.

'Have you been living under a rock?' it asked, punctuated by a string of emojis she had no time or energy to decipher right then. Dr. Crenshaw would have her hide; she still had a few hours before the dragon's shift ended and she left the hospital in Zenobia's hands for the night.

Hours later, finding a lull when the usually overflowing waiting room lay empty, she sat down with a sigh and took her phone out. Her inbox overflowed with messages. Annabelle knew not to call, for Zenobia rang when free from the shadow of her irascible boss.

She started with the first text—'Have you been living under a rock?' had a hyperlink with it. She tapped that without a second thought. Zach's fiancée lived for gossip and tended to be over the top on a normal day.

A track started, notes which sounded African, a little like the opening of the iconic The Lion King song. Then she could make out trills, the sound of water, maybe the sea on a calm beach. Strange how it all reminded her of Mauritius. To be honest, if she hadn't been there recently, she wouldn't have made out the distinction, would've just enjoyed how the music flowed gracefully along. A voice touched the rhythm, a woman speaking, her voice breathy, almost ethereal. A laugh ...

She blinked then frowned. This sounded a lot like ... wasn't that what she'd said to Jaeden in the recording booth of that studio?

The track had been playing window-in-window on her phone. She tapped to be taken to YouTube where it had been uploaded.

And there, staring at her black on white, was the name she'd been trying to erase from her consciousness for the past five weeks. DJ Den.

So he'd used her voice on his music without letting her know? The gall of the man!

Quickly, she returned to her home screen and dialled Annabelle's number.

"What the fuck?" she exclaimed when the woman picked up.

"So you've seen it?"

"Just did! The cheek of that arse. He had no right—"

"Wait. Hold on one sec. You're going to berate him for such a heartfelt gesture?"

In what world did that woman live? "He used my voice on one of his tracks!"

Silence ensued on the line, so stark that she pulled the phone from her ear to see if the call had dropped. It hadn't.

"You haven't read all my texts, have you?"

"Just opened the first and saw this!"

"Aww, ma puce. Read my texts. Please. And look at the comments online."

Something bristled along her spine. "Why?"

"Just do it, okay?"

The call ended then.

With a frown, she went back to the texts. Annabelle had chronicled the whole drama. The timeline went back way over twenty-four hours. What had she meant about the comments?

Going back to YouTube, she scrolled down. That's when she saw it. #FindHerDJDen seemed to be trending, all the posters—except for a few trolls, of course—encouraging him to go after her, whoever this 'her' happened to be. Some had even started discussions among themselves on the hashtag, spreading the word to be on the lookout and sharing all the details they knew about this mysterious 'her.' One poster had referenced a video from where they were getting all their information.

Her heart suddenly hammering in her chest, she tapped the link and was taken to an Instagram page. Jaeden's, to be more precise. One of his Stories had turned into a Highlight.

It must be more than twenty-four hours old.

Her thumb hovered over the little circle, a debilitating apprehension growing inside her the more she stared at this highlight. What would she find ...?

She wouldn't know if she didn't look, would she? So, on a deep inhale, Zenobia tapped the circle and watched the screen blow up to reveal a selfie video of Jaeden which seemed to have been made in a recording studio.

The breath lodged in her throat at the sight of him. He looked tired, almost haggard, deep circles under his eyes. When was the last time he'd slept properly?

Then he started talking, and everything in her froze.

"By now, you must have heard this untitled track that's supposed to be mine. It is. A work-in-progress which should never have seen the light of the airwaves. Not that I don't want to share my work with my fans and followers, but because …" He paused, emotions running over his face. "Because this one was personal." He gave a small smile. "You see, I was recently in Mauritius, and I met someone there. A gorgeous woman, as beautiful inside as she is outside. We had very little time together, but time is irrelevant when your very insides know something." He smiled genuinely this time. "I heard her giggle first. Yes, it's the same one on the track. And I fell in love with her without even realizing it at the time." The smile died. "I don't know where she is now, except that she's in India. The only thing I have of her is her voice and the sound of her giggle which I mixed with other sounds that remind me of her. That song? It's her."

He stopped for a few seconds, his throat working as he swallowed and then clamped his jaw. "I apologize for this debacle that got unleashed on you all. Peace and light, world."

The screen froze on his face, the circular arrow icon appearing in the middle, asking if she wanted to replay the video.

She did, acting on pure instinct, fuelled by the urge to drink in more of him.

Jaeden had just admitted he loved her, to the whole world?

But as she listened to the recording over and over again, something grew startlingly clear.

He hadn't asked anyone to find her for him … He wasn't even looking for her.

How many times can a heart break?

Many, as she was finding out. Wrapping her arms around her bent knees, she hugged herself and cried.

***

Over thirteen bloody hours on a plane. This better be worth it.

Who was he kidding? Nothing would ever be as worthy as this.

Pitch darkness hovered over the surroundings, making this part of India as indecipherable as the Shetland plains in the throes of winter. The car stopped after passing through a narrow entryway that should've been barred by a gate but lay empty. Jaeden gazed up the path to the expansive, flowing circular fountain near the carriageway drive leading to the wide porch of a wooden colonial-style dwelling. Even in the dark, ramshackle would be too generous a descriptive to attach to the crumbling building.

So this was the hospital where Zenobia worked. If he didn't love her so much already that there wasn't much space left for that feeling to grow, he would've lost his heart upon seeing this. Because his Zayn had so much to give that she didn't need much external support and props to be able to do so.

Uncanny how one could figure a person out, their very essence, in so short a time. What a trip love was—in every sense imaginable.

He alighted from the vehicle and stared at the actual fire torches burning along the wide terrace that ran all around the house. Hazardous, what with all this wood. He, however, had to remember not everywhere in the world did the people have the luxury of twenty-four-seven electricity.

A chorus of cicadas reached his ears, lending a lulling quality to the eerie quiet of the night around here. He started walking—after all, he'd come here for a purpose. Up the stairs he went, the floorboards of the terrace creaking under his footfall as he made his way to the lobby that must've been the main reception room in this old house during its heyday.

A man was dozing in a chair to his left. He jerked awake as Jaeden crossed the threshold, and a little bell rang out.

"May I help you, sir?" he asked.

Jaeden nodded. "I'm here to see Dr. Hashemi."

The man gave a nod and motioned for him to follow. He did, going across the lobby, through a string of rooms, then emerging onto a patio that led down to an inner courtyard where a massive tree grew in the middle, a three-foot-tall circular concrete wall all around it.

There she was, sitting on the ledge, her back to him, her long braids a startling contrast against her white doctor's blouse. The flickering lights from a few of those traditional earthen Indian lamps added a soft glow around the place.

He went down the steps, never tearing his eyes from her. When he reached the ground, he continued towards her, stopping less than a yard from the concrete ring. For long moments, he just stared at her. Then, watching no longer felt enough.

"Zayn," he said softly.

She stiffened, her spine straightening. He'd almost heard a gasp.

She slipped to her feet from where she'd been sitting, then turned his way. Surprise registered on her beautiful face, her mouth falling open, confusion swirling in her green eyes.

His heart was beating so fast, he feared it would ram out of his chest at any second. Good thing he was at a hospital.

"Hi," he managed to say.

She blinked. "Hi ..."

When it seemed obvious she wouldn't say more, Jaeden knew he had to bite the bullet and take the first step. He did exactly that, moving towards her.

"I ... I missed you," he said.

She didn't move, looking like a beautiful statue bathed in the radiance of the lamps. The yellow tone almost made her glow like she had that night they'd danced together.

He gulped as he stopped less than two feet from her. He'd come here to tell her something, hadn't he? Best he get on with it.

"How ... how did you find me?" she asked.

He smiled. "Annabelle, and your brother."

Zach had read him the Riot Act over the Skype call before giving Jaeden his blessing to pursue her.

"Jaeden," she started. "That video ..."

"I was hoping you'd see it."

"You ... you meant it?"

He nodded. "Every word."

"You told the world you loved me."

"I did."

"You never told me ..."

He hadn't, had he?

"I love you, Zayn."

He bridged the distance between them and raised his hands to cradle her soft jaw in his palms.

"My poison," he mumbled.

She batted her eyelashes, and a single tear rolled down her cheek. He couldn't bear to see her cry.

"And my remedy," he continued.

Her lower lip trembled. "Wh-what?"

"You're my antimony."

She was a doctor; she'd figure out what he meant, antimony being highly toxic in its right but also used as an antidote for quite a few others in the past.

A hint of a smile touched her face. She'd worked it out.

"I should've told you first," he breathed out. "My fans—"

She placed a hand on his mouth, shushing him. "Music is your life. You should always be allowed to share it."

He could hear she meant every word of that. But she should know how important she was to him, too.

"You're also my life. I'm not sharing you, though."

At this, she giggled. Jaeden's heart soared, his soul singing. He didn't waste any time to swoop in and drink that lovely sound from her mouth as he stole a kiss.

She melted against him, and just like that, the world set to rights.

When they broke apart, he smiled at her, then reached into his pocket and brought out a small box. Without a word, he went on one knee before her.

"Jaeden," she gasped.

Long, silent seconds stretched between them. Then she giggled again.

That was all the answer he needed. He slid the ring onto her hand, then wrapped her in his arms, kissed her, and swung her around.

The sound of her joyous laughter would forever be the most crystalline symphony he'd ever heard.

***

A little while later, Jaeden had propped himself on the railing of the balcony surrounding the house. His fiancée flitted around the main room. Patients had been coming in since dawn had lightened the darkness over an hour earlier. From time to time, she would lift her head and smile at him, and his heart would sing. Because her smile was no longer broken. He'd accomplished what he'd always wanted ever since meeting her.

But he had one more thing to do. Pulling his phone out, he opened his Instagram account and went to the Gallery, finding a cryptic image that a discerning eye would figure out was a Tiffany & Co. ring box.

He selected the picture, captioned it, and posted. He owed it to his faithful followers to keep them updated.

'Found her. Never letting her go' he'd written.

His quest had come to an end. A new adventure now began.

*

ZEE MONODEE

Of Indian heritage & a 2x breast cancer survivor, Zee lives in paradise (aka Mauritius!) with her long-suffering husband, their smart-mouth teenage son, and their tabby cat who thinks herself a fearsome feline from the nearby African Serengeti plains. When she isn't in her kitchen rolling out chapattis or baking cakes while singing along to the latest pop hit topping the charts, she can be found reading or catching up on her numerous TV show addictions. In her day job, she is an editor who helps other authors like her hone their works and craft.

Website: http://www.zeemonodee.com/

When Love Happens

ROSEMARY OKAFOR

WHEN LOVE HAPPENS by Rosemary Okafor

Morgan is ruthless and plays dirty to protect his billion-dollar conglomerate. However, he holds a dark secret that could destroy him if exposed. His relationships with women are about pleasure alone until one weekend with the beautiful Eno leaves him ready to risk everything for her.

Eno was a young journalist when she witnessed Morgan murder his wife. Six years later, she's ready to do anything to make him pay for his crime. Until she falls for his charms. Now she's torn between destroying the proud billionaire and allowing herself to fall in-love with him.

CHAPTER ONE

"Are you ready for this?"

Eno adjusted her headset and muttered gibberish into her mic.

"Can you reduce the volume a bit?"

This would be the second time she would be seeing the Abuja business mogul. The first time had been six years ago at Sheraton Hotel—she was starting her career as a journalist and had gone to Abuja with her boss to see him about the murder of his wife.

"Say something. Let me take your level," Eric, her camera man, instructed. "Okay ... perfect." He confirmed with a thumb up.

No matter how long she had done this, interviews like this made her nervous.

"It is not every day one gets to interview Chief Morgan Cookey." Eric threw her a glance with an encouraging smile.

"I know, Eric." She ran her fingers on her dreadlocks plaited into a Mohawk and adjusted her glasses closer to her eyes. "I just don't know what to expect ... It is difficult to know which question is appropriate."

The hot weather was beginning to grease her T-zone, making her glasses too heavy for her small nose to carry. She removed them again and wiped her nose with her palm before replacing them. The thing balanced better on top of the bridge, and she wiped her sweaty palms on her dress.

"It is no different from interviewing Dangote and Otedola. This is your beat, Eno. Why are you nervous?"

"I have met this man before. Believe me, he is different from the two you just mentioned. He is a monster."

"How did you figure that out? Have you spoken to him before?" He glanced at her again, bemused. "Okay, you actually have to calm down. You are practically freaking out. You will be fine"

"Really? I mean ... is it that obvious?" She pointed at her face.

Eric dabbed his hankie on her face. "The meeting will soon be over, and he will be out any moment. I wouldn't want you to ruin my video."

"Thank you, Eric."

The pandemonium around them announced his emergence. Journalists straightened themselves, arranged their gadgets, and pushed their way forward as the door to the prestigious Presidential Hotel Reception flew open and heavily armed men swam out first before he stepped out between them.

None of them had planned for the silence that followed his emergence. To Eno, his aura was still as intimidating as it had been twelve years ago. The only time she had felt that aura was six years ago when she was in Lagos to interview *Charlie Boy.*

Chief Morgan cleared his throat and flashed one of the most amazing smiles she had ever seen before the *click clicks* of the cameras came alive.

"Proud bastard," she muttered. He was a handsome man, with a demeanour that was nothing but ruthless.

"He is good. It's like he was born for the camera," Eric added.

"Chief, what is the fate of the Baran Rafi community dwellers whose lands have been taken for the construction of your mega headquarter?" She broke the silence, emphasized *'your.'*

He turned and rested his gaze on her—the most intense look she had received. His eyes scrutinized her for a few seconds before he smiled.

"Wilson's Group is a company that is people-oriented. The wellbeing of the people is our concern, and we will make sure the organization improves the lives of citizens at all cost," he replied.

"But is the organization ready to dialogue with the community concerning their lands which was taken from them?" she continued.

He gave her another long look.

"I don't know about 'taking' any land. The community was well consulted before we started construction on the land, but rest assured that we are going to meet with the aggrieved faction of members to settle the matter amicably," he answered, giving her a knowing glance before he continued. "We are not the enemy of the community. We have done so much when it comes to development both in Abuja and other places. Our work speaks for us in Lagos and Enugu."

"How long are we going to wait for your company to fix a meeting with the aggrieved members of the Baran Rafi community? From the information we gathered, they said they have not received any news nor any compensation from your organization," another journalist added.

"Like I said earlier, there is a faction that feels they deserve more." He chuckled, his rich, curly beard giving his face a formidable look. "You know Nigeria. One cannot please them all."

He gave a quick glace towards where she stood. "The issue of compensation was settled two months ago. However, we will continue to foster peaceful coexistence. We will sit with the aggrieved members."

"He is good ... very good at masking his true self," Eric whispered to her.

"Hmm," she agreed.

"I have to retire now, gentlemen of the press ..." he was saying.

"How are you coping with the vacuum left by your late wife, and are we expecting a wedding soon?" she asked before she could stop herself.

Chief Morgan turned to her sharply, squinted up at her, and mockingly asked, "Are you applying to fill the vacuum?"

This evoked laughter from the crowd.

"It has been a long day," he added in finality before he tore his eyes away from her and hurried down into his car.

"That was spontaneous," Eric said while folding the cords.

She gave out a wheezing breath she hadn't known she'd been holding since Morgan had given her the sharp gaze. "Let's get back to the office."

***

"Such a nerve," Morgan muttered.

"Yes, sir. I couldn't believe Alhaji Mumuni would look you in the face and ask for an increase after what was agreed. Maybe he feels you are young and can be pushed around."

"Hmm ..." He agreed with his driver who had become family even when his father, Chief Sese Cookey, had still been alive. He was a good man who'd served his father for fifteen years and had remained with him twenty-one years after.

But he wasn't thinking about the meeting he'd had earlier, nor the swarm of media people that fought to devour him. But the young journalist ... he was sure he had seen her somewhere.

"That lady journalist. She is a fearless one," he said with a chuckle.

"Yes, sir. Too fearless for her own good."

And it fascinated him. In fact, he had been drawn to her the moment she'd asked the first question. He knew how intimidating his presence could be. He had been told about that often, but the lady hadn't been shaken by this.

This would be the first time he'd ever taken a long, interested glace at a woman after the death of Fatimah six years ago.

"Ah! Fatimah," he muttered.

She had been his world, the only woman who'd understood him perfectly. Theirs had been love at first sight, her boldness and her intelligence drawing him to her.

"What man blushes like a woman ... you are turning red!" she had commented the first day he'd met her at the hospital in Amsterdam. She was the daughter of the then-minister for works and on her annual routine medical check-up while he had visited a doctor friend.

They'd ended up becoming friends from that day and had graduated to lovers few months after. It hadn't been difficult for her to accept his proposal even though he was a Christian.

Then the fights had come.

"You are never around, Morgan. What do I do with myself?" Fatimah would cry out.

The female journalist reminded him of her. Her last question had brought back the guilt and the pains he had tried to hide. Yet, there remained something striking about her.

"I like her," he said.

"Sir?"

"The female journalist. She seems … interesting in some kind of annoying way."

His driver looked at him through the rear-view mirror. "You have not talked about liking a woman after Fatimah."

"I can't talk about any woman the way I talk about Fatimah."

"It's been six years, sir. I am sorry, sir. I shouldn't remind you—"

"Set up an appointment with her at my office," he cut in, then picked the newspaper beside him. "I will give her all the interviews she wants."

He had a mischievous smile while he turned the pages of the paper—relationships with women had become flings after the death of his wife. But maybe things were about to change.

CHAPTER TWO

"The interview is smooth as usual."

"Thank you, ma'am."

Eno's boss pulled a drawer and brought out an envelope.

"I heard you indirectly applied to become Mrs. Morgan Cookey." A pen hung loosely between her lips.

"It wasn't exactly what you ... I didn't intend it to be understood that way," she defended herself.

"Well, you ended up messing up good work. Have you checked the evening dailies? It has something juicy about you ... and that is not good for this organization."

"I am so sorry, ma'am. It wasn't intentional, please."

"You have a good sense of humour, Eno, but most times, you don't know when to cut the jokes and mean business."

She opened her mouth and closed it as words disappeared from her tongue.

"I am afraid your carelessness may cost you this job someday."

"My sense of humor gets the job done most time, ma'am," Eno blurted out.

"If you want to be a comedian, you can apply for standup comedy with Ali Baba. Journalism is a serious business."

"I have always done my job with positive results. Does it matter what strategies I use to get the answers I seek?" She lifted her brows and looked suggestively at her boss who gave her a long stare.

The boss knew she was right. Somehow, she had gotten some of the toughest men smiling at the camera and singing like birds while she interviewed them.

"May I remind you, young lady, that I call the shots here. I am the one sitting here and you are—" she waved her fingers towards where Eno stood, "—you are the one standing over there."

As Eno worked hard to suppress her anger, the other woman gave a satisfactory smirk. "Here. Your allowance."

"Thank you, ma'am."

Her boss dismissed her with a wave of hand.

Eric followed her down the stairs and handed her a copy of '*This Day*' newspaper.

"You are in the spotlight once more," he said.

She snatched the paper from him and continued walking.

"Let me guess, you argued with the boss again." Eric was running out of breath as he struggled with his bulky figure to meet up with her.

"She doesn't like me." Eno shoved the paper under her armpit and balanced her weight on one leg, her gaze searching the road for a taxi.

"She hates your guts," he said in between heavy pants.

She looked anxiously at her watch. It was getting dark, and soon, it would be difficult to get a taxi around that area.

"I could give you a lift with my bike, you know," he offered.

"No, Eric. As much as I want to jump at the offer, I don't want you to have problems with Ma'am."

She gave him a smile, and he smiled back.

"You know I can do anything for you, Eno ..."

"That shouldn't include losing your job."

"I can always get another one. I am an engineer …" He came forward to hold her hand.

She heard the sound of an oncoming vehicle and hurriedly pulled her hand away from his grip to wave down the taxi.

"Where?" the driver asked.

"Moshood Abiola Road."

"Enter."

She sat at the back and clutched her handbag to her chest while Eric closed the door.

"See you tomorrow, my lady," he said.

He always called her that, especially the times he wanted to profess his undying love to her. Some of those times, she would allow herself the pleasure of laughing to his poems of love, but tonight was not one of them.

As the taxi navigated from Constitution Avenue towards Independent, she rested her back against the seat and closed her eyes. It had been an eventful day. Her mind strayed back to the interview earlier.

She could swear Morgan hadn't just looked at her. His gaze had lingered as if he had something against her. But she'd also seen something else in his eyes.

She turned her face away from the street light and opened her eyes.

Six years ago, she had been at the same hotel where his wife had been found dead. She'd seen him pull the knife out of the dead woman's body and throw it behind the flowers before he raised an alarm. Four months later, he had invited her boss to Abuja and had paid heavily to help him clear his name and get the news out of the papers.

"Is this man not supposed to be behind bars for murder?" she had asked her former boss.

"He is a powerful man, Eno. That's what they do ... clear their names with money—" they had been visiting every media house, social media their second home, their eyes red for lack of sleep just for this murderer, "—and our job is to give them the image they crave for ... get our money and off we go," her former boss had said.

She had wished Morgan would pay for his crime.

"We don reach Moshood Abiola o." The driver turned towards her.

"Oya go right, then go left again, I dey go Emeka Anyaoku Street," she said with a yawn.

"You for tell me since na, your money na five-hundred-naira o."

The estate was unusually quiet. Even the men that sat by the entrance and argued about Biafra and Nigerian government most of the nights were not at the gate, where only two security guards sat idly. One flashed a torch light on her face, and she shielded her eyes with her hands.

"Aunty ... you come late today o," he commented before letting her in.

As she walked towards her apartment, her hair stood on end, and fear gripped her. She was sure she'd heard footsteps, but when she turned, there was no one following her. She picked up her pace, clutched her bag tight, and pushed her glasses closer to her eyes to prevent them from falling.

After her investigation and publication of the activities in the power sector, which went viral and led to further investigation and sacking of Billy Dickson, the Minister of Power, she had always had the feeling that she was being followed.

'You don't know me ... I will waste you ... I will make sure you never write anything in your life again'

That was the message she got three days after Chief Dickson was sacked. She had reported it to the police, but she had no way of proving who had sent the threatening message.

She heard a soft whistle and rapid footsteps behind her. When she turned, she saw a figure coming towards her. Eno didn't wait to know who it was. She picked up her skirt and ran.

The house welcomed her with a musty smell immediately as she opened the door. She switched the light on, sank her buttocks on the only sofa in her one room, self-contained apartment, exhaled with her mouth, kicked her shoes, and looked around the room.

"What is happening to me?" she muttered.

How could she convince anyone about what was happening to her when she wasn't sure if it was all her imagination playing some tricks on her?

"One day, I will leave this place to somewhere more comfortable."

She rubbed her left elbow with her palm and walked towards the window. When she opened the curtain and looked out, she saw no one.

Getting a decent house in that side of the town came with money she couldn't afford even after twelve years of working as a journalist. The riot in her stomach reminded her that she had not eaten anything after the cup of tea before leaving the house.

She opened her refrigerator but found only a left-over yogurt and a piece of cake. She shook the yogurt before she drank from the container, smacked her lips, and took a bite from the cake. Then, she walked back to the sofa with them. She was still adjusting herself on the seat when her phone rang.

She ignored it at first, but when the call persisted, she picked up. "Hello?"

"From Wilson Group ..."

Eno sat straight immediately. "... ehm ... what? I mean yes ... alone? I ... I will."

The line went dead before she could ask any question.

***

"She will be here tomorrow." A statement.

"Of course she will. Is she not a young journalist hungry for stories to push her career?"

Idris placed the phone in his breast pocket. "Why are you interested in her, sir?"

"The question is ... why is she interested in me?"

"Have you met her before?"

"That, I intend to find out."

Idris understood the air of finality in those few words, and he didn't push it. "I will be heading home now, sir. My family has not seen me for three weeks now."

"You are traveling back to Zaria this night? Haba Idris! Sleep over at the house today, and go first thing tomorrow morning." He suddenly felt lonely.

"No, sir. Aisha will be angry with me. I promised her I will return to her today." His face lit up with a smile. "Besides, it is her birthday today."

"Ah! And you didn't tell me," he accused the old man. "It's already eight p.m., and you cannot get to Zaria in two hours' time by road."

"True, sir, but—"

"Mallam Idris, you can have the chopper for your journey. Put a call across to Captain Mark. He will see to it that you get to Zaria on time"

"I am grateful, young sir. Aisha will be happy."

"Tell Aisha that I miss her and will make time to see her and the children."

"Catch some sleep, young sir. You are working more than your body system can carry, and that is not good for you."

A little sting of envy needled its way through him as he watched Idris close the door behind him as he left. He was lonely, and he couldn't cloak it anymore. Unlike Idris, he had no one to return to. His mansion has suddenly become too big for him. He had tried keeping the girls in the mansion with maids while he flew round the world, though.

"You have to get a wife, Morgan. No maid can replace the function of a mother," his sister had advised him at a point.

"I cannot subject any woman to the kind of loneliness I subjected Fatimah. It was loneliness that drove her to her death," he had replied.

He had resolved to take his daughters on some of his business trips until he couldn't do that anymore and his sister took them with her to Ukraine.

How alone he felt …

CHAPTER THREE

"Follow me, he is expecting you."

Eno had hardly been able to sleep throughout the previous night.

Why does he want to see me?

Twice, she had wanted to call Eric and tell him about the invitation, in case anything happened to her, but she'd decided against it. *Eric would insist on coming with me*—a bad idea.

It was as if he had told everyone of her coming, "The Journalist ..." They would give her a nod while she moved with the man who'd introduced himself as Jacob.

Two uniformed men stood at both sides of the entrance door to the room she later realized was his office. They straightened up as they sighted Jacob.

"Wait here," Jacob said to her and walked inside the office. He came out few seconds later. "He will see you now."

He held the door while she walked in.

"You are seven minutes and four seconds late," Morgan said without looking up from the papers on his table.

"I encountered a little traffic on my way. I am—"

"Late ..." he cut in, and looked at her finally.

She said nothing, but she held his gaze, and this made him drop the paper he held, relax his back on the chair rest, drum his fingers on the well-polished wooden table, and lift his brows.

She looked away.

"I am sorry," she muttered.

He buzzed the intercom on his table, and a beautiful middle-aged woman entered the office.

"Tea?" he asked with his eyes on her.

He was studying her, and he knew she was aware.

"Just water," she replied.

"Two cups of tea please, Mrs. Portia." He ignored her objection, pushed his chair backward. He stood up and walked towards the sofa.

"Join me," he said, and walking ahead of Eno. He sat and waited for her to sit before he spoke. "Have you been here before?"

"No," she said, and he smiled.

The cups of tea arrived. He took one from the tray and sipped leisurely, savouring the taste, and licked his lips to the excitement of the middle-aged woman.

"Mrs. Portia, you are the best tea maker in the world," he said while giving Eno a mocking glace.

Eno looked away. Mrs. Portia giggled.

"Oh, you think I am lying? My guest can equally testify."

Smooth ... so smooth, mister. But I am not going to fall for your charm, Morgan.

"Have a taste, Eno. Tell Portia what a good tea maker she is."

Eno looked from him to the poor woman waiting for her compliment. She took the cup of tea and had a sip. She wasn't a tea lover, but it was good, she couldn't deny that, so she took another sip and nodded before she swallowed. "It's nice ... really nice."

His face lit up in a big smile, and he looked at Mrs. Portia. "I told you."

Mrs. Portia smiled back and looked at both of them in appreciation. "Thank you, ma'am. Thank you, sir."

She picked the tray and left.

They drank the tea in silence, observing each other while forming opinions.

"How did you get my number?" she asked.

"And your name," he added, before picking a cookie and shoving it into his mouth. "You don't like cookies? These ones are good," he offered.

She said nothing.

"Well," he continued. "I have my ways of getting any information I want about anybody." He ate more cookies. "As long as I pick interest in the person."

His gaze fell on her chest. Her blouse had a 'V' cut neck which exposed the upper part of her breasts.

She swallowed hard and pulled the neck of her blouse up. "What else did you find out about me?"

He drained his cup and relaxed his back with his hands spread on the arm rest. "Well ... nothing too interesting. Your life is as boring as mine. You have no life outside your job."

"I have a life," she said between clenched teeth.

"Oh?" He raised his brow. "Tell me about it, then. The last time I checked, you still move around with that over-bloated camera guy in search of stories by the day and come home to an empty house in the night," he said with a smirk on his face.

"How dare you? How dare you say such a thing about me? Who do you think you are? How dare you bring me here to humiliate me?" Anger raged in her, and seeing him keep his cool with that mocking smile at the corners of his lips made her want to slap his face.

"And are you any better?" she continued. "You think this whole place—" she gestured with her hands, "—the front you are trying to put up, your charities

... you think all of that can make up for your brutality?"

The smile wiped off his face.

"You murderer!" she blurted out.

His face darkened. "What did you just call me?"

His voice was deadly calm. As she realized how far she had gone, she didn't care. What mattered to her was to tell him what she thought about him.

"You think we have forgotten how you murdered your wife at Brantford Hotel and sent the police on a wild goose chase? How you paid every media house to cover your stinky past? I was there ... I saw you pulling the knife off her body."

Panting, heaving, anger flared from his eyes.

"So that was why you asked the question about my loneliness the other time. You wanted to rub the guilt on my face. You were there to taunt me—"

"I was there to do my job!"

His anger poured on her like burning embers. Afraid he might hit her, she got up and took a few steps backward.

"It all makes sense now. I know I have seen you before ... you were the girl who came with Bolaji six years ago to my hotel room."

She said nothing.

"Why did you work for me if you saw me commit the murder? Why didn't you write about it?"

"I need more evidence before I can break the walls of lies you have built around you," she answered.

"You never believed I was innocent. You questioned me with all the bitterness in you. Even when Bolaji pleaded with you to let it slide, you never did. I saw it in your eyes then." He turned his back on her. "I see that now."

He walked back to his table and sat down.

"Get out!" His voice was ice cold.

She didn't wait for him to say it the second time—she picked her hand bag and left.

***

Why had he kept the truth away from the public?

"The scandal will not be good for your reputation and your business," his lawyer had advised him when the police had been on the case. "Tell them what is necessary."

How would he have told the world that he wasn't man enough to keep his wife happy? Every media house would carry the story of his wife's preference for another man. He had gone ahead with his lawyer's suggestion, the secret kept among immediate family members. Fatimah had been murdered by men who had been blackmailing her because she was committing adultery. He would never have known— she had threatened to not pay up, so they'd killed her? The scandal would've been bad, but he'd been thinking about his children. That's why he'd done what he'd done.

He opened his window blind with two fingers and watched the journalist as she walked out from the gate. She brought out her phone and probably punched a number before she placed it to her left ear. He wondered who she was talking to, thought of ordering his men to bring her back for a search in case she'd had a camera on her.

I am a fool. He should have known better than to be so careless around a journalist. A taxi stopped before her, and she entered.

He pulled a drink from the fridge, poured some in a glass, and gulped before he dialled Idris.

"I have to let it all out. The guilt is killing me."

CHAPTER FOUR

'I want to see you in my office today. 4pm will be fine. Morgan.'

"Bastard," she muttered and deleted the message before settling on her sofa with a mug of black tea. Her phone beeped again after a few minutes; another message from the same number. She sipped and picked the phone.

'You can come with your man friend if you want. A first-hand information on the death of my wife won't be bad for your organization'

Liar. Who knew what lies he wanted to come up with this time?

Then her phone rang.

"Eno!" Eric blurted out. "Where have you been?"

"Eric, I am not feeling too well. I couldn't get up from the bed yesterday," she lied.

"Oh my God! Should I come over ...?"

"No!" she shouted. "No. Eric, please don't bother too much. I will be fine in a day or two," she said mildly.

"I was worried about you. You didn't say anything to anyone. You didn't pick my calls or respond to my messages."

"Oh my goodness! Eric, I am so sorry. I had wanted to reply but totally forgot."

"That's okay. So should I come over after work? I can bring dinner ..."

She sensed the plea in his voice.

"Oh, okay, but seriously, you shouldn't bother at all. I will be—"

"I want to do this, Eno. I like you a lot, even though you don't like me ..."

"Eric, please, don't do this now ... you know I like you. Okay, you can come over after work."

"I have to go now. Madam has been bellowing since morning. I think it has something to do with your absence."

She felt Eric's excitement and smiled.

The phone went dead before she could reply. Eric was a nice guy, the only staff that hooked with her immediately after she was employed. Both of them had worked together for three years, and unfortunately, Eric had developed a thing for her.

***

The soft knock on her door woke her up. She rubbed her eyes and stretched her body. The knock came again, this time louder. She jacked up, looked at the clock, and hurried to the door.

The person pushed her inside and shut the door. She landed on her buttocks, wanting to scream, but the intruder was fast. He covered her mouth with his large palm, his index finger slipping inside her mouth and his nails piercing her palate.

She fought while he held her to the ground and struggled to bring out something from his breast pocket. She bit his finger, pulled herself backward, and kicked his face. Eno then staggered to her feet to run.

"Bitch," he muttered, spat on the floor, and ran after her.

She wrestled with the toilet lock until the hook fell on the tiled floor and gave her away. She gasped, her hands on her mouth. She threw her weight on the old door, but it was useless as the intruder yanked the panel off its frame and pulled her out by her hair.

"You have a message from Honorable," he said harshly.

"Please! Stop, please!" she sobbed as he dragged her back to the room which had become a wreck. "What is my crime?"

"You journalists think you can write anything and get away with it ..." He pulled a pocket knife from his pocket. "When you have no fingers, you write no more."

He forced her down to the floor.

"No, please! Don't do this! I am begging you!"

Ignoring her, he spoke with someone on the phone "I have her ... okay ..."

He shoved the phone in his pocket and bent over Eno, his knee spread over her.

They didn't notice when the entrance door opened and someone walked in.

"What is happening here?" Morgan's voice was a harsh whisper. He hurried towards the intruder and pushed him off Eno.

"You bastard!" He threw a punch, and the attacker landed on his back. Morgan threw himself on the man who was trying to get to his feet and held him by the neck.

"What are you doing here? Who sent you?" he bellowed.

"Morgan!" Eno called out as she got to her feet.

A few neighbors had gathered, and the police had arrived. They took the man away, forcing him inside their van.

One of the policemen approached them. "Thank you for alerting us, sir. We will take it from here. Can I ask what brought you to this place at this time of the night?"

When Morgan gave him a stare, he stuttered, "Sorry, sir ... It is none of my business, sir ... Just that—"

"I will see Inspector Jonah in the morning, Officer," Morgan cut in.

"Right, sir."

***

"How did you know?" she asked.

They were in his car, heading she had no idea where as he had not explained to her yet.

"We need to get you out of here," was all he'd said to her before he'd taken her hands.

"I was stalking you for real now."

He tried to make light of the situation, but she didn't laugh. His yellow shirt was rumpled and stained. Part of her wanted to touch his bruised face and thank him, but the other part held back.

"Why did you show up? What do you want from me, Chief Morgan?"

He glanced at her and looked away.

"Take us to Maitama," he said to the driver.

"Yes, sir."

They rode in silence for a while before he spoke without looking at her.

"I wanted to see you, to speak to you concerning ..." He looked at her. "Concerning my wife."

He drummed his fingers on his lap for a moment, and she let him gather his thoughts.

"I wanted to tell someone what actually happened. I don't know why it has to be you, but ... well, I guess I came just in time to save the day." He gave a sigh of relief. "I guess you don't know those men?"

"Men?"

His words had taken her by surprise.

"There were three of them. Two were outside." He gave a weary smile. "You have made some enemies. Any idea which of them would want you dealt with?"

Even with mild bruises on his face and a swollen lip, he was handsome. *How can someone evil look so beautiful?*

"I don't know…" she muttered.

"A bitter ex, then." It was a statement.

"It has something to do with my job." She caught his attention with those words. "The report I made concerning the power sector last year."

He gave out a surprise gasp.

"It was you!" He looked her up and down. "Why am I not surprised! You have got some nerve—"

"I am only doing my job, sir."

"Of course you are." He pulled his eyes away from her. "Well, if you are right about who is behind this, we should find out and make sure he gets himself off your back permanently."

"Thank you." she said.

"That is the first 'thank you' you have said to me since I came to your rescue."

Heat bloomed on her cheeks, but it didn't seem like he expected her to respond.

"… And you are welcome," he added.

He walked her into the house she believed was his, showed her to a room.

"My sister stays here whenever she visits." He looked her over. "Her clothes can fit you, so … make yourself comfortable."

***

Morgan didn't know why, but he felt like staying with her. She looked so vulnerable yet so strong. It had been so long since he'd felt like gathering any woman in his arms and whispering comfort in her ears.

"Buzz the telecom if you need anything. The house keeper will attend to you." He made towards the door.

"Ehm ... Chief Morgan ..."

"Hmm?"

"I am really grateful. I just want to say thank you."

She stood with her locks loose and her eyes on his face. She had beautiful eyes, he just noticed.

He walked towards her, took her hand, and placed a phone on her palm. "I forgot to give you this. It's what brought me to your house tonight."

He covered her fingers round the phone and walked out of the room.

He scratched his head and touched his swollen lips before he settled inside the car. "We are going to make the news tomorrow morning, Idris."

The driver brought the car to life. "You did a good thing, sir."

"So did you."

CHAPTER FIVE

"I was afraid you would be gone by the time I came back." He allowed himself over the threshold. "Maria said you have not left this room since morning."

"I can't leave this place even if I want to." She stood up from the arm chair and paced the space.

"And why is that?"

"Haven't you seen the news?" She grabbed he phone and brought it to him "Look at this! They think we are having a secret affair!"

"Are we having an affair?" he asked with amusement.

"How can you even ask me that? We can never have an affair!"

He eased himself from the door and walked towards her.

"Do you hate me so much, Miss Eno?" He closed the gap between them and held her shoulder. "When you look at me, do you see a monster? A dishonorable man?"

She opened her mouth and closed it, blinking a few times before she turned away from him.

"If you had met me in a different situation ... maybe you would have longed to have an affair with me." He took some strands of her locks and let then drop on her back. "You fascinate me, Eno ... I want to hate you as much as you hate me, but—"

"I don't hate you, alright!" she cut in "Not after ... I went through the phone you left with me last night."

He left her and sat on the bed. "So what now? What do you think of me?"

"I don't know what to say ... I am sorry."

She felt awkward standing there, her emotions in turmoil. His presence made her lose herself. She'd thought she could look at him like any other man, but he was different. She'd had it all wrong about his wife; she could see that now.

"I, ehm ... I have to go."

"But it is late!"

She shuffled the contents of her hand bag and brought out the phone. "Here, I should return this."

He didn't collect it from her.

"Why?" he asked.

She dropped the phone on the bed. "Because it belongs to you."

He picked the phone, fiddled with it for a while. "Was it useful?"

"I don't know what to say ..."

"So how soon should I expect the news to make the head line?"

Making the conversation as formal as possible, he slipped the phone into his pocket and faced her.

"From me? It is not going to happen." She zipped her handbag. "I am not going to write anything about it, it is ... too personal."

The words were choking to her, so she swallowed and continued. "I am so sorry for ever accusing you—"

"I don't want pity from you, not from anyone." He cut in harshly, his voice as cold as dead ash.

She shook her head to prevent the tears from streaming down.

"I am ... sorry," she sniffled. "I have to go now."

She headed for the door.

"Eno."

The sound of her name from his lips made her stop. She heard him approach and felt his hands on her shoulders.

"Stay, please," he whispered close to her ear.

A sob escaped from her throat.

"I want you to stay with me." He turned her to face him.

"Why do you want me to stay here? Why?" she asked.

"I don't know. I just want you around. Maybe I can finally give a name to what I feel inside about you." He smiled.

"This is not right. I shouldn't even be here in the first place," she muttered.

"Yet, you don't want to leave. I can see it in your eyes."

His eyes searched hers. Without warning, he gathered her in his arms and took her lips with his. He held her as if he half-expected her to fight him, but she didn't. When he gently pulled away, he looked at her as if waiting for her to say something. She licked her lips, took her bag, and turned to leave.

"Eno ..."

"I have to go, sir."

He let her go—that was the best thing to do to save both of them.

She was grateful when Idris offered to take her home.

"Thank you, Idris," she said before she sat in the car.

As he was about to close the door, her eyes caught Morgan looking at her from the window. She swallowed hard and glanced away.

"Are you alright, ma'am?" Idris asked.

"Hmm ... yes ... sure." She touched her lips and closed her eyes until he announced their arrival to her house.

***

"Where were you for two days? Two days, young lady!"

Eno had reported to work the following day with little hope of not being sacked. The looks from the other staff had already told her she was in for serious trouble. Eric was not in the office when she came in; he had gone in the field with Joan, the new girl in the marketing department told her.

She had hesitated before she tapped on the chief editor's door and quietly pushed the panel open when she heard the loud bellowing from the office. She suddenly felt pity for the junior editor all the insults were being hauled on while he stood like an abandoned mannequin.

Her chief editor turned her aggression on her, providing the already deflected junior editor an opportunity to escape from the office.

"I took ill," she answered.

"How can you take ill at this time? Why will you take ill and keep my organization on hold?" Her eyes were bloodshot for lack of sleep. Eno felt pity for her, too.

"And why didn't anyone inform me about this your sudden taking ill?"

"I informed Eric, ma—"

"Eric?" she cut in "Who is Eric? Is he the management?"

"I am really sorry, ma'am."

"In this place, there is no room for frivolities and stupid excuses. You work because you have to work, and you must be available anytime you are needed, or you find yourself out of this place!"

"Yes, ma'am."

"Get out of my office and make yourself useful!"

She was almost at the door when her chief editor called her back.

"We got information that Federal Government will be meeting with major business stake holders next Wednesday." Her boss pointed a pen at her. "Find more about this arrangement and prepare for it."

While she sat at her desk reviewing reports that came in minutes ago, she kept glancing at her phone. She desired that somehow, she could get a message or a call from him, but deep down, she knew their encounter had ended last night. He hadn't called to inquire how she got home …

She had waited half the night.

CHAPTER SIX

"... the federal government has instructed the Central Bank to release Forex at one-hundred-and-ninety-seven naira as against three-hundred-and-sixty naira for the importation of materials which will aid means of production. Let it be known that the government has decided on banning the importation of some specific goods and services ... the listed items are in the papers handed to everyone ..."

The Minister for Economy was making his speech when she sighted Morgan. She had lifted her head from her writing pad when their eyes met and he looked away. She wasn't so sure, but she felt his gaze had been filled with admiration which vanished as fast as it had gotten there. It took her few minutes to put herself together and focus on the meeting.

"He is here," Eric, who had busied himself with taking pictures immediately since they'd arrived, whispered behind her.

She was startled. "Who?"

"Our man, of course. Who else?"

"Oh." She pretended not to take interest.

"Are we going to block him for an interview after this?" Eric asked.

"I think it will be better to go for the minister. After all, he is representing Mr. President here."

She didn't want to face him. It seemed obvious from his attitude that they no longer had anything to discuss.

It was over.

***

Morgan had restrained himself many times from calling her, but he'd been uncertain about what she would think of him. He had searched for reasons to give her to explain his call, but all had sounded lame. The truth was that he missed her, the fire in her, her anger that made him want to laugh. The few moments they'd spent together had suddenly brought life back to him. Some days, he would remember her and laugh alone in the car with Idris stealing a glance at him from the rear-view mirror.

"That lady journalist. Did she call my office while I was away?" he had asked nonchalantly on one of the days Idris picked him from the airport.

Idris had looked at him and cleared his throat. "Was she supposed to call, sir?"

"Oh, she doesn't have access to my office. Even if she did, the secretary would have answered."

Idris had driven him in silence from the airport straight to his mansion.

"You miss her, sir," he had said before handing his briefcase over.

Morgan had denied it, though, but as the cold air from his room hit his face and he balanced his briefcase on the floor while he sank his buttocks on the side of the bed, he knew he couldn't lie to himself. He missed her.

He'd been half-expecting to meet her at the stakeholders meeting. He had rehearsed his reaction if he eventually saw her, but nothing had prepared him for the beauty that graced his eyes and how his heart jumped into his stomach when he set his eyes on her. She wore her locks packed up and folded like a bulb. He felt too old to be having such feelings for any woman, and it made him ashamed.

***

She was pushing her way towards the front to get a clearer statement from the minister when he stepped out from the venue. He kept glancing towards her while exchanging pleasantries with other stakeholders before he walked with his General Manager to the car park.

He meandered his way around the camera men and got to his waiting Lexus, his latest car. His love for cars dated way back, even when he was just nine years. He had known the names of almost every vehicle and could identify any motor brand by its sound even when it was out of his sight.

He gathered his white Agbada and sank into the back seat while Idris closed the door. He moved his head forward in search of her. Idris waited patiently for him until he wound the window up.

"To the airport," he instructed.

They rode in silence. He signed papers, answered calls, checked his laptop, until he lay his head on the headrest, placed his palm on his forehead, and grimaced.

"You need rest, sir. Can I drive you home rather?" Idris offered.

"I have to be in Lagos for a board meeting by four p.m."

Idris parked the car by the side of the road and turned towards him. "The board meeting can always be rescheduled, but your health cannot wait. I am not taking you to the airport, son. You are going home."

"I have no home, Idris," Morgan muttered in pain, but he made some calls nevertheless.

Idris smiled and resumed their journey home. He kept observing Morgan in the rear-view mirror.

"Why don't you call her?"

"What?"

"The journalist. You like her, you know. I saw the way you looked at her before we drove off."

"I am tired, Idris. I want to rest."

***

Eno had already retired to bed when her phone beeped.

'Come away with me tomorrow night, lady journalist. Idris will pick you up seven pm. Morgan'

She jacked off the bed, her heart panting heavily. She shouldn't be feeling this way for him.

Another message came. *'Again, you were beautiful today'*

What is he doing? What does he want?

She dialled the number, and it rang for a long time.

***

He had typed and deleted before being able to send the ones he did, but he couldn't get her off his mind. Her eyes ... her soft skin ... He'd thought he would forget, but seeing her today had reinforced his desire for her. He turned and tossed on his large bed.

His phone rang. Eno.

"You found me," he mused aloud.

"Why are you doing this?" she asked.

"Doing what?" he teased her.

He is aware of how he makes me feel, he is taunting me. He sounded tired, yet his voice made her feel weak in a sweet way.

"I saw you today. You are beautiful, Eno." The way he whispered the name, she shook her head, shut her eyes as if to fight what he made her feel. *Calm down, Eno,* she thought to herself.

"I saw you, too, Chief. You—"

"I couldn't get my eyes off you."

His voice sounded alluring. She could imagine his eyes on her, caressing her skin. The thought of it gave her a tingling sensation.

"I … I didn't realize," she managed to say. She had concluded he was obviously ignoring her.

"So, what do you say?"

He cut into her thoughts.

"About what?"

"Come away with me tomorrow night."

With the way he made her feel, she was ready to go anywhere with this man even if she may never see him again after that.

"I … am working tomorrow. I may work late." Her tongue had grown heavy; she suddenly became a stutterer.

He hesitated. She could hear his heavy breath from the other side.

"I don't remember the last time I begged for anything, Eno, but I am begging you to just give me one night. Tomorrow night, and I promise never to bother you again."

She had her back against the wall, her legs folded. She picked the pillow and hugged it tight against her breasts. She lacked words to say to him. Just one more time to look at his lovely face, one more time to hear his laugh and see him lift his eyebrows at her, one more time with him could make her lose every sense of self-respect and demand to be kissed by him. Didn't he know that? Why did he want her to yearn for him? Was he punishing her?

"Please, little lady. Don't turn an old man down."

It made her chuckle.

"I am almost thirty-three, and you are not that old," she said and laughed.

"Glad I can make you laugh."

"Please stop—"

"So what is it going to be, darling?"

Darling? He'd called her darling ... She didn't know what to make of it, but she liked the sound of it.

"I ... ehm ... okay ..."

"That will do. I will send Idris to you."

She was nodding her acceptance as if he were there with her.

"Okay," she whispered.

"Sleep now, little lady."

It would be one of those nights she would turn and toss on her bed. She would reminisce about every word he'd said to her and would smile to herself. The feeling was so much that she feared she would wake up to realize it was all a dream.

CHAPTER SEVEN

"I was thinking ... Can we go out tonight?"

The next day crawled like a slug. Eno kept looking at the time and anxiously watched the sun while trying to put down whatever Hajia Kudirat Abdulazeez was saying.

"You are losing concentration, Eno," Eric has commented, worried for her. "Are you okay?"

"Yes ... yes."

"You have been checking the time since we got here. Are you expecting someone?"

How crazy would it sound if she told Eric she was going on a date with the same man she had portrayed as terrible, and that the same man had succeeded in turning her into pudding that would melt away just by the sound of his voice?

"No. Just ... feeling like the day should just come ... to an end." She returned her eyes on the notes she had already taken. Eric must've sensed the excitement from her voice, but he didn't comment about it.

They worked in silence for a while, with him trying to engage her with his witty remarks once in a while.

"It's my birthday, you know," he said casually.

He was hurt—she sensed it in his voice. How could she forget how important his birthday was to him? She looked at him with guilt that must surely be written on her face.

"I am so sorry, Eric. I totally forgot about your birthday!" She took his hand, gave it a little squeeze. "Happy birthday to you, my dear friend."

Her smile made him smile. He finished folding the wires, wiped the camera aperture, and shut it.

"I was thinking you could ..." He stole a glance at her and looked away coyly. "You could spend the evening with me ... you know. We can watch a movie. I just don't want to spend today alone."

He heaved a sigh then, the look on his face said he was hoping she would agree to his request.

She opened her mouth and closed it, blinking several times before she exhaled from her mouth. "Ehm ... Eric, I don't know what to say. I mean, I ..."

"Forget it, I understand. You wouldn't want to be seen with a whale like me."

He walked towards their waiting car, and she ran after him.

"No. No, please, Eric, wait." She caught up with him. "Look, it is not what you think."

It was obvious he would not hear whatever explanation she had to give, as he kept walking.

"I am sorry, Eric, but I already have plans for tonight." He said nothing, "Okay ... I will go with you."

She blamed herself the moment she uttered those words.

His eyes lit up, and he smiled broadly. "Really, Eno?"

"Hold on, now." He had already hugged her; she gently pushed him away. "Only if what I planned for tonight doesn't work."

He hesitated before speaking. "Okay, I will deal with that."

He was smiling like a child, but she felt pity for him.

She wished she'd never uttered those words, making her confused about what to do. What if Morgan showed up?

He may not show up, anyway. He is always busy, she rationalized, trying to make her situation easier.

Eric was coming every now and then to check on her.

"I am going through a directory of nice places. I want the perfect place for you," he would say one time.

"Oh, you know this downtown takeaway restaurant? I heard they have good fried chicken. Maybe we should go there," he would say another time while he walked from the editing room to the store.

By closing time, he had a taxi waiting downstairs for both of them.

She picked her bag, threw some faint makeup on her face, and hurried downstairs to meet him. But she came face to face with someone else.

"Idris!" Her heart jumped out of her chest.

"He sent me to get you." He looked from her to the big man waiting beside the taxi. "Is he waiting for you?"

"Yes. No. Let me go talk to him." She didn't know how he would take it, knowing how touchy Eric was. He was already seated inside the taxi when she reached him.

"Eric, I am really sorry. I thought he wouldn't show up."

"It is him, right?" He wasn't looking at her.

"What are you talking about?"

"You think I wouldn't recognize his car or his driver anywhere?" His anger and self-pity were now tangible. "I knew he was the one. I saw it on your phone!"

"What? Eric! How did you get my phone? How dare you go through my phone?"

But Eric was beyond reasoning.

"I have wanted you to see me, to love me. I practically did everything for you ... I saved you from losing your job when you were busy fucking the old man!" His voice had grown high.

"Hope there is no problem here," Idris said behind them

"Ehm, no, Idris. Let's get out of here."

"You are now familiar with his driver? You call him by his name now?"

Eno left him shouting in frustrated anger and walked away.

***

"He is your colleague."

"Yes." She had not asked where they were going to. She'd just wanted to get out, away from Eric. She couldn't believe he could do this. Was he stalking her? How ... When did he take her phone?

"Miss Eno, I don't mean to pry, but ... do you have anything going on with him?" Idris watched her from the rear-view mirror. "The way he was shouting at you, I was wondering ..."

"Believe me, Idris, there is nothing going on." She turned her face towards the road. "I know he has always admired me, but ... believe me, there is nothing more to it."

Constitution Avenue was unusually crowded that afternoon.

"It's Friday. Jumu'ah," he said as if he'd read her mind.

"Oh, right." She gave her thumb a little bite. "Idris?"

"Hmm?"

"Where are we going?"

He smiled at her through the rear-view mirror, and she smiled back.

"To your house first, so you can get dressed, then to a place he would rather I keep secret." His smile lingered.

She bit her lip and turned her face towards the window, suddenly forgetting what had gone on between her and Eric.

"You love him," Idris said.

"What? No!" She was laughing "Okay, yes. I like him ... A lot."

"I love young love."

"We are not so young, Idris."

They both laughed.

***

"How do I look, Idris?"

The old driver was having the time of his life. He remembered when his daughter Zara got married last year. "*Daddy, how do I look?*" she had asked.

"You look beautiful. I know my son will not keep his eyes off you," he replied the anxious Eno.

That was the fourth dress she'd tried out that night, her bed now filled with dresses and her box opened and kicked aside at the corner of the bed.

They drove off towards the airport.

***

The taxi that had followed them came back to life when they drove a few yards away, Eric didn't know where they were going to, but he was determined to carry out his revenge. There must be something that would get him the sweet moment he sought.

"Oga, it's like they are going to the airport o." The taxi driver was getting impatient and worried.

"Follow them."

"What do you mean, 'follow them'? How much are you paying me for this?" he lashed out.

"Any amount you want." Eric had wanted to spend so much on the woman he had loved. But that had been before the feeling drained from him and left him with bitterness and the desire to ridicule her before everyone. "Just follow them. I will pay you handsomely."

They drove the almost free road in silence, only the broadcast from *We FM Abuja* warming the interior of the taxi, not that Eric was interested in the broadcast, anyway.

"Sir, we no fit pass here o."

"I will handle it." They were at the first gate that would lead them into Nnamdi Azikiwe International Airport.

"Where to, sir?" The security guard peered inside the taxi.

"I have a late flight to catch ... I am running late." Eric looked straight, then at his watch, and gave the security guard a questioning look.

The man hesitated before he removed his head from the taxi. Hitting the body of the vehicle, he said, "Okay, you can go. Safe trip to you."

CHAPTER EIGHT

"Idris, I am curious now. This is the airport, and there is no one in sight."

"He is here. Look." Idris pointed towards the silhouette of a man walking down towards them, with his hands in his pockets and a charming smile on his face. "I will leave you now, ma'am."

Idris quietly left her side.

"My God! He is handsome!" she said under her breath.

She wouldn't have given a man his age a second glance, let alone think of going on a date with him. But she would die to have the man advancing towards her. As he closed up on her, nothing else mattered except the both of them.

"Cat got your tongue?" he said amidst a chuckle, gently removing her jacket. He eyed her up and down before he fixed his gaze on her face. "Perfect."

His tone depicted lust, and she could see hunger in his eyes. She couldn't hold his gaze for long, so she lowered her lashes.

"You are shy," he said seductively and lifted her face with his middle finger. "Look at me, Eno," he whispered.

What she saw in his eyes sent desire down her spine. She felt so helpless standing so close to him that she didn't know what to do with herself.

"You sure you want to come with me?" His eyes clouded with desire, he searched her face. She nodded, but he wanted more. "Say it, my little lady. Say you want to come with me."

"I want to come with you … Sir."

"Morgan."

"Morgan."

He gave her a broad smile, brought his fingers to her lips. Her heart started to beat faster. Thinking he was going to kiss her, she parted her lips, but he only whispered in her ear.

"I like how I make you feel."

Oh, God! This was one of the most careless things she had ever done. What if someone saw them? They were in an open place, and he was a public figure. He may have nothing to lose, but she … she may not be able to show her face in public. Also, what if this man lured her there to kill her for the secret he had shared with her?

"Are you changing your mind?" he asked.

"No."

"Good. Come, we have the whole weekend ahead of us." He offered his hand.

***

"Disgusting old fool," Eric spat in disdain.

He adjusted the aperture and took as many pictures as his distance could allow. It wasn't easy to get that close to where the two stood. He had almost given up until he got lucky and met a security guard who believed his lie.

"My wife came here to meet another man. I have been a good husband and father to her and the children. Now she wants to abandon us to travel with another man."

"Sir, call her line now. You are not allowed any closer to the hangar," the guard suggested.

"She will not pick my calls. Please let me see her."

"Here, use mine." The guard offered his phone to him.

"No sir, it is no use," he sobbed. "She would not pick."

He sniffled and wiped his nose with the back of his hand.

"Do you know the man?" he asked the guard.

"Which man?"

"The man that my wife has gone to meet."

"I don't know the one you are talking about. There are so many men that come in and go out here. Besides, I am new here. I don't know regular faces yet."

Eric had carried on with his pity show as the guard led him out. As the man took the other direction, he got his opportunity to go back from the exit terminal towards the hangar. While he took the pictures, he kept looking back for sign of anybody approaching his hiding place.

When he meandered his way out, he ran as fast as his bulkiness could allow him towards the waiting taxi.

"Let us go," he instructed the driver.

The taxi was at Tasha Road when he flipped his digital camera and scrutinized the images he had captured with a simper. He pulled his phone from him pocket and dialled a number.

"I have juicy photos you may want to look at ... Yes ... You will not turn away from this one."

***

"Did you love her?"

He threw a piece of fried shrimp into his mouth, chewed lazily, and glanced at her. "I used to."

"Now?" She threw pebbles onto the beach. He had brought her to his beachside cabin in South Africa.

"I want to be with you alone, away from the cameras," he had said to her when she'd asked where he was taking her to.

To her amazement, it was a beautiful house with only three bedrooms. He had read her surprised look when they'd walked into the house.

"This place has always been my place of escape, when I wanted to go away with my ..." he'd paused. She was sure he would've said his wife. "My family," he'd added rather.

The house held so much memories, the pictures of his two daughters and a big framed picture of his late wife. She'd felt a little stab of jealousy. *He still loves her*, she had thought as she'd stood in front of the smiling, beautiful woman.

"Fatimah," he had referred to his late wife. "I kept the picture because of the children. They shouldn't forget their mother entirely."

He had then taken her hand and given it a reassuring, gentle squeeze.

"Now, I don't feel anything." He sat up. "I used to feel angry because of what she did to me, then I started feeling guilty ... I blamed myself for years for pushing her into what happened. I punished myself for her death ... that was why I didn't want to talk about her, or her death, with anyone."

She gathered her legs close to her chest and lay her head on her knees.

He continued. "I have learned to heal; I now understand that people make choices, and ... someone else shouldn't be blamed for that."

He relaxed his whole frame on the wooden chair, exposing his naked thigh to her discomfort. Since they'd arrived the previous night, she had tried to avoid intimate contact with him. She had imagined him without anything on many times, but she wasn't prepared for the arousal his bare torso and thighs could give her. From a distance, she had managed to curb her lust for him. It became a difficult task for her to pretend that he wasn't there with her, the close contact, having to deal with bumping into him with a towel round his waist and wet hair curls from his chest that disappeared under the towel, leaving her to imagine what it covered.

He was looking at her again, and she dared not return the gaze for fear of what she might see.

"Do I make you uncomfortable?" he asked.

"No. Just that ..."

"You are suddenly quiet, darling." He moved close to her, and she shivered. "You are cold ... Maybe we should go inside."

"No!" she cut in. "Sorry. I mean ... I am okay."

She was safe as long as they discussed business, tourism, books, and her job. They had much in common, she'd found out. He was a man who loved books.

"My collection of books can make a whole school library," he had boasted over dinner.

He took pleasure in talking about his chains of businesses, and she listened. "Do I bore you?" he would ask.

"Not at all. I can write a complete two years' monthly magazine on you and your business," she had joked.

They had also talked about her.

"Do you have a man?" He'd squinted at her.

The last man she had dated had gotten tired of her busy and boring life and moved on with someone more fun.

"He is a fool," Morgan had said calmly, and she had smiled.

"How do you feel about me, Eno?"

His question took her off guard, bringing her back to where they were at the moment. She hesitated at first. He had his hand round her neck. His skin was extremely soft and made hers respond.

"Ehm, I don't know … Maybe …" She couldn't find the right words.

"Should I tell you how I feel about you?" He turned her face to his. She felt his warm breath and his gaze on her lips. "Has anybody told you that you have sensual lips?"

His husky voice made her body stand with desire.

"I have tried to be sensible with you for a long time, Eno. I don't know how long I can withstand seeing your sexy body without going crazy."

She moaned.

"God! This woman!" He bent his head and took her mouth with his. He caressed her lips in a most beautiful way, deepening the kiss as he parted them with his tongue. He gave a throaty moan, gripped her back tight, and pulled her towards him.

"I can't get enough of you," he murmured.

He traced his way down to her neck, gave her skin mild bites, and nibbled on her ears. She went crazy with pleasure; she could feel the enlargement of the bud of her womanhood and her wetness made her flimsy underpants sticky.

"Morgan …" It was a moan.

"My little lady … You have turned me into this."

He laid her roughly on the sand and gave the bulge of her breast a bite before he released one from its cage, the firmness of her nipple seeming to drive him crazy.

"Eno!" He gave out a throaty cry, introduced his tongue to the nipple, circling it while she wiggled in pleasure. "Tell me what you want, my lady ... I want to hear you say it."

He licked the tip of the nipple and gave her a look.

She couldn't take the torture anymore, so she grabbed his head with both hands and pushed his mouth down to her breast. He welcomed the offer with hunger, sucking and licking while he had the other hand on the other breast.

Both were carried away by the pleasure of the moment. Nothing mattered anymore. Not the press, not their age difference. The wind caressed their bare bodies, the rushing sound from the beach consuming their moans, the throbbing of his erection against her hip heightening her pleasure.

"I want to make love to you, Eno ... here and now," he said. "Please, darling, let me make love to you."

He stopped moving. With his eyes on her face, he pleaded.

It took that split second for her to realize how vulnerable she was under him. She became ashamed. Ashamed to give herself so cheaply to a man she barely knew.

"Oh my God!" She pushed him off her and staggered to her feet. With tears on her face and her bra loose, her breast bare, she ran blindly towards the cabin.

"Eno!" he shouted.

She couldn't stop. How could she allow herself to be used? He'd never said he loved her. Everything about the whole thing, the trip, was just for his pleasure. She stumbled, and he caught her.

"Eno, please ... I am so sorry. Please, my darling, I am sorry."

She shot him a look, roughly wiped her eyes, and ran into the cabin, shutting the door that led to her room behind her.

CHAPTER NINE

"Who is this guy?"

Their secret rendezvous made the news Monday morning, the picture of them holding hands, smiling at each other. His picture had been captured perfectly, obvious that whoever had done the job had been accurate about his timing.

'*Struggling journalist gets herself a billionaire*' was on the front page of the *Nations* newspaper.

'*Few days after she subtly indicated her interest in becoming Mrs. Morgan Cookey, the multi-billionaire owner of Wilson Group, Ms. Eno Ikot has succeeded in securing the money bag as the young journalist from the Voice newspaper has been seen going in and out of the Ivory Tower where it was gathered that she has no official business with the widowed CEO.*

According to an undisclosed source, Ms. Ikot had kept her illicit affair with the billionaire a secret and away from her fiancé until she could no longer keep up with her game.

The aggrieved fiancé was seen exchanging a heated argument with Ms. Ikot who stood him up on a date and flew to a weekend gateway with her prince ...'

"I think I have seen this guy ..." He pointed at the full coloured picture of Eric beneath Eno's.

"The camera guy that works with her, sir," Idris said carefully.

"What? How is this possible? How could she lead me on when she has someone?"

"Don't take it so hard—"

"Don't tell me not to take it hard, Idris! She deceived me … she is a liar!"

He paced around in his office, bumping against table and sofa. The door opened, and Eno walked in with a copy of the newspaper in her hands.

"Is this true?" His voice was as cold as death.

"Morgan …" she started.

"Answer me! It this shit true? Did you ever date this guy?" he shouted at her.

"No! No, Morgan. Yes, he liked me. He asked me out, but—"

"You dumped him! Because you wanted to make your way into my life. You planned it all. You cheated two men!"

"It is not true!" she sobbed. "Please don't say those words to me …"

"I should've known who you are from the beginning." He was lashing out at her. "It was all about the money to you."

"Please, Morgan … I can't do anything to hurt you."

"You hurt me, Eno. You hurt me real bad." He came towards her and pointed at her face. "I don't want to see you ever again, not around here, not anywhere near me … Not anywhere!"

She sniffled, wiped her tears haphazardly. "I actually came to explain to you, but it is obvious there is nothing to explain. I want you to know that … I am sorry for everything. I guess I didn't know where I belong. I should have known it would never work between us."

Fresh tears streamed down her face, and she roughly wiped them off. "Thank you for judging me like the others. Thank you for believing them without listening to me."

She grabbed her bag and ran off. Idris looked from her to Morgan, shook his head, and walked after her.

***

"Eno, open the door." She had waved a taxi down before Idris came out. He must've come after her. "Please, Eno, open up."

"Go away, Idris. I don't think I can do this anymore," she answered, her voice broken in sobs.

"Let me see you, Eno. I want to talk to you, please."

She hesitated before she let him in, then she went back to the bed and buried her face in the pillow.

"You love him." Idris ran his hand on her locks.

"It doesn't matter now," she said angrily.

"I know he loves you, too, but—"

She turned sharply and faced him. "He doesn't love me. If he does, he would have protected me. That is what lovers do!"

"He is foolish. He doesn't know what to do at the moment ..." he said calmly. "Please forgive him, my daughter. Give him some time. He will reason properly."

She jumped off the bed.

"Well ..." She grabbed her box and threw it on top of the bed. "By the time he comes back to his senses, I should be gone."

She stumbled towards her wardrobe and gathered her clothes at once, then dumped them inside her box. "Tell him not to bother about me anymore."

He watched her without saying anything, then he quietly left her apartment.

***

"I though you are wiser now. You are as foolish as when you were a child." Idris met Morgan in his office.

"That is an insult, old man, and I won't have you do that." He didn't look up from his computer.

"How can you feel so strongly for someone and abandon them when they need you most?"

"I don't know what you are talking about."

"Well, if it matters to you … She is leaving Abuja today. You can decide to continue in your misery."

With that, he walked out.
***

He'd thought he would have felt better. Revenge was supposed to be sweet—why did he feel this emptiness? Why did it hurt so much? Eric scratched his beard absentmindedly; it was Tuesday morning, and the news story was still the topic of discussion on every media channel.

"Why do you want to do this?" his editor had asked him, giving the footage close scrutiny.

"I think it is newsworthy. If we run it, it will generate huge sales and traffic to our social media platform," he had lied.

"It is good." The chief editor had given a nod, her eyes still fixed on the footage.

"Thank you, ma'am."

"I will get it down to the printing department once I am done here," she had assured him.

He'd been heading for the door when she had stopped him.

"One more question, Eric." She had paused, looked him in the eyes, and asked, "Did you actually have anything intimate with Eno?"

Rather a lie-detecting question.

He swallowed, battered his eyelids several times. "Yes. We were supposed to make it official next week, before ... before she ... he ... she chose him over me."

His lies had formed a huge lump on his throat and almost choked him.

"So, what is this about? What do you want from this?"

He couldn't provide a concrete answer to that question, but the organization had gone ahead to run the story anyway, and it had broken the Internet and had gotten wild responses from readers. He had trended this few hours. Some media presenters and bloggers had made this look like a poor helpless boyfriend whose love had been snatched from him while others had called him a cry baby.

'The lady in question is an adult who knows what she wants, if she doesn't want you...why cry over it?' A participant on *Kakaaki* AIT show had said.

He grabbed his phone. He'd expected several phone calls from Eno or even messages. He wanted to know her reaction, how she took the whole scandal. He went through his call log and messages for the umpteenth time, and his face registered his disappointment.

'Up until now, Chief Morgan has not made any formal statement on this scandal. He has refused to even grant an interview to the press on this ...'

"Smart man," Eric muttered and turned the television off.

***

"I am foolish."

He ran his fingers on his beard. It was Tuesday night, and he had not seen her nor heard from her. He tried her line again—switched off. "Where could she be?"

He had suddenly become miserable just the few hours after she'd left his office in tears. He felt like beating himself. "What is wrong with me?"

"Sir, a call for you." His personal assistant walked into his study with one of his phones.

"Who?"

"Your sister. She said it is urgent."

He took the phone.

"Speak," he said with no interest.

"I have been calling you on your private line, and you have ignored me." She feigned anger.

"Mary, please. I am not in a good mood—"

"You are in the news again, brother."

"Again ... How many times have I trended in the past years?" His voice held scorn.

Mary snorted at him. "So who is this lady who has dragged my brother under the prying eyes of the media?"

"I ... Just a lady I met, but it was over as soon as it started." He combed his beard with his fingers.

"Then you should know how to deal with the media and move on with your life. Idris told me that you have been sulking since Monday. What is wrong with you?"

"I don't know. I am worried about her. I ... ehm ... I have tried calling her, but she has refused to pick my calls. I went to her house and—" he sighed, "—she's moved out."

His voice had grown subdued.

His sister hesitated before she responded.

"You feel something for this lady?" She chuckled.

"I don't know. It's all confusing. I think I like her, you know, but ..."

"So, what is the issue here? I don't get it, Morgan. How is it possible that you cannot interpret the feelings you have for a woman?"

How could he have allowed his pride to come between what he'd shared with her? He loved her; he could no longer ignore that. The fire in her eyes, the sound of her voice, her laughter, and her anger. The weekend they'd shared had been one of the best moments he'd had in years.

He picked his private phone and checked for a response to his messages. None had come in.

"What have I done?"

CHAPTER TEN

'Is it enough to say I am sorry?'

She read his messages for the first time as she kicked her shoes off and placed her earrings on the table beside the bed in the modest hotel room. His messages raced in immediately as she turned her phone on.

'I was being foolish. Call me anything you want and I will accept but please my little lady, forgive me'

She hissed and walked towards the wardrobe to unpack her box. She had planned to go see her father but had decided against it. He would want to know what had brought her back when it was not Christmas or a public holiday. She couldn't lie to the old man; it would be useless to try, anyway. Her father would always get the truth out of her.

She didn't know how long she would stay in the hotel; she didn't have so much to pay on hotel bills, but she'd needed a place where she could be alone and cool off before making any other decision.

'How do I make it right? Tell me what to do and I will do it. Please Eno I am sorry. I was proud and couldn't stand another man's claim to have been with you. I was dying of jealousy, but I have known better. Please my love'

She deleted his messages, sat on the bed, and with her hands covering her face, she cried. She couldn't hate him no matter how much she tried. Yet, she couldn't allow herself to continue with what they had. He didn't trust her. In fact, he disrespected her. She'd pleaded for him to give her a little of his time, to hear what she had to say for herself, to protect her, but he hadn't. He had condemned her and thrown her out.

Her phone beeped again, and it was from him. Her head warned her not to read, to delete like the others, yet her heart spoke louder.

'*I can't hide this anymore. You are the best thing that has happened to me in years. You haunt me Eno. You are here in my head and my heart. You gave me one of the best experiences when you were with me. I didn't know I could still feel for any woman how I feel for you. I don't want to lose you my darling. I have searched for you everywhere I know. Please come back to me...*'

She gave out a sob. With her palm covering her mouth, her shoulder rocked with the stifled sound.

"Morgan, please leave me alone! I can't do this with you," she cried.

Her phone rang. This time, she picked up but said nothing.

"Where are you, my love?" Through the first thing he said, she could sense the relief in his voice. "Eno, please come back, or ... tell me where you are, please."

"Why?" She shut her eyes, and hot tears ran down.

"Why? My darling, I want you. I have not been able to do anything with myself. You took my happiness with you—"

"Stop! Please, Morgan. I don't want to hear any more." She wiped her face. "It's about you, right? It has always been about you ... You, Morgan, whatever will make you have ... your royal highness." Her voice rang with sadness.

"Eno, it is not true—"

"Hold on! Please let me finish. These few moments have been ... We have done everything that pleases you. I won't deny that ... that they weren't memorable to me, but I can't do this anymore, Morgan ..."

"Eno, don't do this. I am begging you, please."

"I begged you, Morgan! I begged you to reconsider, but you didn't. You didn't think of me when you chose not to believe me ... You never cared, after all."

"Eno, I had no idea ..." He sounded bewildered. "Don't you have any feeling remaining for me? Can't we start all over again?"

"Sorry, Morgan. This is the end. Please."

She cut the call before he could say anything.

"Don't you have any feelings remaining for me?" he had asked.

It wasn't just a feeling but love that she had for him, and it scared her. How could she deny that he didn't make her happy? He had brought out the wild and adventurous side of her, had trusted her with his life and his secrets; they had created memories together. His body against hers had aroused her like no other. He had treated her like a queen, his queen.

"What have I done?"

***

He didn't call or send any text the next two days, not that she'd been expecting him to do so. She placed the last pair of shoes in her box, zipped up, and balanced it on the floor. She looked around for anything she might be forgetting. A soft knock came on her door.

"Hold on!" She had told an attendant to come for her luggage. She opened the door and froze.

"Do you think you can hide in this city without me finding you?"

His baritone voice sent chills all over her. His gaze lingered on her before he cast it on her already packed box. He walked into the room and shut the door behind them.

"How could you break up with me like that?"

"We ... we were not dating ..." she answered.

"Oh." He lifted his brows. "I didn't realize."

She faced him. "What are you doing here, and how did you find me, Chief Morgan?"

"First, to find the woman I love and bring her back to me. As for how I found you ... I told you I can get anything I want, especially when I have an interest in the person, and you, my darling—" he gave out a wicked smile "—I am interested in."

His eyes now challenged hers.

"Tell me, Eno. Tell me, do you think you can actually walk away from me just like that?" His eyes softened, and he sighed. "Tell me that you don't feel anything for me, Eno, and I will walk out of here and never bother you again ... Tell me that I mean nothing to you, that what we shared was just for that moment alone."

He moved closer to her, held her arm, and brought her body crashing onto his. "Look at me, Eno. Look at me, please."

She did.

"How can you deny this? How can you deny us? What I see in your eyes ... what we felt when we kissed. How you called my name and moaned when I touched you ... Tell me they are all lies."

She looked away from him.

"Morgan." It came as a whisper. She fought not to allow him to break her with his words.

"You arouse me like no other woman has done. You turned me into a boy meeting his first love." He took her hands and placed it on his chest. "Feel the rhythm, my love. My heart beats for you. Tell me you don't feel the same way."

She shook her head. "I can't ... I am confused."

He bent his head and took her lips in a kiss. She moaned. She had kept her hands down. As he deepened the kiss, she wrapped her hands round his neck and closed her eyes. There was hunger in his kisses. He wanted more so he took—parting her lips, he took her tongue in his mouth and drank from it.

"Morgan ..." She was breathless.

"Tell me you missed me, for I missed you terribly ... I am sorry for letting you down."

She knew she wanted this man. She didn't know what to call the desire both of them had for each other, the lust for his body enough to make her do anything to be by his side. Yet, she wanted something tangible, something concrete, something that would last for a long time.

She gently pushed him away. "Morgan ... what we have isn't enough for me. This attraction scares me. I can't live with it alone ..."

She turned her back on him.

He held her from behind. "What if I offer something more? What about love? Is that enough?"

"You don't understand." She wanted commitment, and he was yet to comprehend that.

"I love you, Eno. I don't know why it took me this long to realize that, but ... I want to be with you for the rest of my life." He placed his head on her hair. "I may not be the perfect one for you, but ... I want to make you happy. Please, Eno. Let me love you."

She relaxed her body. "I am scared ... I—"

"I will protect you, my love. Just tell me you love me, and I will take care of everything."

She turned to him, "Are you by any chance proposing to me, old man?"

"Probably, my little lady."

His eyes were filled with love and admiration for her. She smiled, her face hot as she hit his chest and pushed herself away from him.

"What now?" He threw his hand on his hips and tilted his head to one side in frustration.

"You have not apologized to me for what you did." She sat at the edge of the bed with a subtle smile on her face.

"I have done that over and over again..." He walked to her. "Come on, woman. Don't be like this."

He spread her legs, knelt between them, and held her waist.

"Do you enjoy punishing me?" he asked seductively.

She nodded "A little."

She bit her lower lip and chuckled.

"You are my darling." He stood up and pulled her up from the bed. "Come, let us go home. I want to make love to you in my bed."

She laughed heartedly "No, sir. We are not married."

He bent his head towards her neck and gave a playful bite.

"We will get married tomorrow," he muttered to her pleasure. Moving from her neck to her collarbone, he teased her with his tongue.

"Okay. Morgan ..." She tilted her head, exposing her shoulder for more. He gave her another playful bite, and she laughed, gently lifting his head. "I am also sorry, Morgan ... Sorry for everything I have put you through."

He gave her a soft kiss. "You did nothing wrong to me, my love. I am the one that has wronged you."

Her face lit up. "I love you so much, Chief Morgan Cookey."

Morgan chuckled.

"And I don't think I will get tired of loving you … So, are we going home, or should we finish it here?" He held one of her butt cheeks and gave it a little squeeze. "What is it going to be, my love?"

He lifted her gown and traced the curves of her butt.

"Sexy," he whispered.

"I want to be in your bed tonight, old man," she said seductively.

"Yes, my lady." He kissed her eyelids and picked her bag.

"Wait! People will see us."

"I don't care. What matters is us, my love."

They stepped out of the hotel, to the blinding flashes of the cameras and the aggressive struggle of audio recording gadgets. Her box was left for the lanky hotel attendant to struggle with—he nearly tumbled upon it.

Morgan had his hand round her waist as they walked towards his car. Tomorrow, they would trend, but this time, she would happily read what the media would put up out there. She had found love, and that was what mattered to her. She was shy, but he held his head high, smiling boldly and looking at her face.

ROSEMARY OKAFOR

Born in Nigeria in 1987, Rosemary Okafor graduated from Rivers State University and has since been employed as a broadcaster, news writer, radio script writer, stage play writer and a shop keeper. She writes short romance and other genres on social media for her followers. This would be her first official published prose. When she is not writing, she is busy as an online marketer, a wife and a mother.

Twitter: https://twitter.com/OziomaRosemary

Until Morning

MUKAMI NGARI

UNTIL MORNING by Mukami Ngari

Following a devastating relationship breakup, Zawadi is out on a girls' night out with friends when she meets a sexy stranger with a deep soulful voice created for baby-making music, the handsome face and hot body of a potential cult leader and who rides a motorbike like a speed demon. He becomes her first one-night stand.

Soon she discovers the sexy stranger is her new investor, Gerald. Things deteriorate when he pretends he's never met her and then she discovers his unfathomable secret.

Will love win this Valentine season?

CHAPTER ONE

January 2018

"Damn, he could start a cult with that body ....
and that face," the lady in the purple dress sitting
next to Zawadi whispered.

Zawadi Juma shrugged and flipped the next page
of the East African. She leaned down and engrossed
herself in the newspaper so the woman could take a
hint and stop talking.

"I would join that cult," the other one next to her
said. The two of them leaned towards Zawadi as they
giggled.

Zawadi rolled her eyes. She'd been out taking a call
when the alleged thirst trap of a man had passed by
the lobby.

"Did you see his eyes?" Purple Dress Lady asked.

Zawadi blatantly ignored them. She was not here
for chitchat, thank you very much; the business plan
on her lap proved that. She was here to make the
investor of this venture capitalist firm fall in love with
her business.

She didn't know much about this person, not
having found a lot about him online except that his
venture firm was called Arcadia and that he had
moved back to Kenya a few months back and was
investing in a couple of Kenyan start-ups, SMEs, and
tech firms.

She needed this pitch to go well. Her company,
Rolla, was scaling so quickly, and she needed enough
money to sustain demand.

Hers was an event-organizing company popular with Nairobians. Much like the famous Blankets and Wine, it appealed to them because she and her team always delivered, they never compromised on quality, and their prices were what Nairobians called 'bei ya mwananchi'—Swahili for the average citizen's price.

Rolla offered one event per month, and tickets sold out as soon as word went out. The theme for the previous month had been Wakanda, and top African acts like Wizkid had performed.

Zawadi looked at her business plan. She had everything she needed to make this meeting a success. She had not slept last night as she memorized her pitch and double-checked her numbers. She felt she was ready now, and she looked like a boss lady in her navy dress and nude-coloured heels.

There were five entrepreneurs before her, each apparently as anxious as she was. She could tell.

They were probably talking about the mysterious hot guy to calm their nerves, because from the way they described him, no one that hot existed, except ... She bit her lip as she remembered two nights ago.

She wiped the grin from her face and reminded herself to focus. Purple Dress Lady had been called in, and within a few minutes, it would be Zawadi's turn.

She started fumbling through her handbag looking for her business card when the receptionist with the close-cropped hair and smiling face approached.

"Miss Zawadi," she called.

Zawadi rose promptly and followed her. She cursed inwardly when she remembered that she'd left her business cards home.

They passed a couple of offices until the receptionist knocked on a mahogany door, the corner office.

"Yes, come in," a voice said.

The receptionist opened the door for Zawadi, who clutched her handbag tighter.

She walked in and immediately stumbled on her heels as she turned back to the door, which the receptionist closed behind her at the same time.

She had to get out of here. Reason being, there before her, hunched over a laptop, was the sexy stranger from two days ago.

Her first one-night stand.

She flushed as a memory of her riding through the city on his motorbike in nothing but his overcoat came to mind.

He had not seen her face yet. She quickly reached for the door handle.

"Miss Zawadi?" he called.

She froze, wishing she were invisible. Then, she took in a deep breath and turned around.

"Have a seat please," he said.

She sat down and tried to look different, and serious.

He looked amazing in his form-fitting, three-piece black suit, and a smile tugged on his full lips as he urged her to sit down.

"I saw your business plan. Very impressive. I was just going through it one more time."

His eyes twinkled with just a little bit of the mischief that had appealed to her two nights ago. This was going to be one intense, uncomfortable meeting for her.

"Gerald." He offered her his hand.

The same hand that had been spanking and squeezing and moulding her ass that night.

"Ah, pleasure." She hoped she did not sound breathless. "I mean, pleasure to meet you."

He nodded, and she wanted to punch herself.

"Is this business a full-time venture for you, or do you manage it on the side?"

Zawadi knew all the answers—they were her life—but the only thing that came to mind was that ride they took through Nairobi before he made love to her under the stars.

"Miss Zawadi?"

"Err, yes … It … It's a full-time venture."

She had quit her six-figure job in a microfinance firm for this.

"Good. How much do you pay yourself from this business?"

"Thirty percent net."

He wrote the number down. "Do you have any other investors that I should know of?"

"My parents own forty percent," she said.

"Well, I need you to buy them off. Is that possible? It's too early to give away that kind of equity," he said and looked her dead in the eye.

He seemed different. His eyes were honey brown. That night, they had seemed dark. Then again, it had been very late.

She also realized that he gave no indication that he knew her. He did not mention it, and his actions did not betray that he did. Was it possible that sexy stranger didn't remember her at all?

She didn't think he did.

"Is that possible, Miss Zawadi?"

"What?"

"Is it possible to buy them off?"

"Yes … yes." Her parents would understand. They always did.

"Alright, then. You have a deal." He extended his hand for a handshake.

He had a firm grip. Just like he had grasped her waist that night as they danced in the club until their bodies had been slick with each other's sweat.

"I will have the paperwork prepared," he said.

"Okay" Zawadi rose up. There was so much going on in her mind, and she wanted to get out of here as soon as possible.

"Let me walk you out."

He stepped away from behind his desk. Zawadi's breath hitched as his familiar citrus musk assaulted her senses. He opened the door for her and walked her out of the office.

"I look forward to doing business with you, Miss Zawadi."

"Sure." She knew she sounded rude, but she was too shocked to care.

Thump, thump, thump, her ears drummed as she walked back to her car.

What had just happened? What had that been?

She'd gotten the deal she wanted, but he had not remembered her.

It had been the most memorable night of her life. Every part of him would forever be etched in her mind ... and he did not remember her.

He had made love to her under the stars, and he did not remember her.

Was she really that forgettable?

Was that the reason Nelson had left her and run back to his ex?

She wound her hands tighter around the steering wheel as she remembered the ring in Nelson's suitcase.

Last month had marked their three-year anniversary. So when she'd found a blue tanzanite ring in his suitcase, she'd known he was ready to propose, and she'd been ready to settle down with him because she loved him.

But then, he had spun her world on its axis when he'd told her that he was moving back to Durban, alone.

He was from Durban and had come to Kenya as a consultant for one of the new oil companies in Turkana.

And now, he said he was moving back home. A week later, he had posted a picture of him and his ex-girlfriend Kate on his social media. Zawadi had put a painful two and two together when she'd seen the blue tanzanite sitting on Kate's finger.

A car hooted, and she realized she had been driving at full speed and had almost collided with an oncoming vehicle.

It only takes one second to make the wrong choice. Not only did she remember her road safety training, she volunteered as a road safety trainer for the city council.

She slowed down her Subaru Impreza and reached for her handbag and her ringing phone. It was her best friend, Pendo.

"Did you get the deal?" Pendo asked.

"Yeah."

This was what she had prayed for all month, but she was not ecstatic about it. She felt like she had fallen in an alternate reality where the men in her life were douchebags.

Maybe she was overthinking things. Pendo used to say she was an over-thinker, and who gets mad because their one-night-stand cannot remember them?

It's supposed to be a one-night transaction, anyway.

Maybe the sexy stranger, Gerald, was doing her a favour. He was pretending he did not know her to save her dignity so they could start their professional relationship on a clean slate. That made business sense.

"What's wrong? You don't sound happy about it," Pendo asked.

"Nothing. I'm super excited."

Damn good friends, she couldn't hide anything from Pendo.

"Meet me at Ichigo for lunch. I'm buying."

"I—"

Pendo hung up before Zawadi could cancel.

Pendo had always been relentless since they were teenagers. They'd met on their first day at St. Mary's Secondary School, both the youngest and tiniest in their class. The long green skirts they wore as school uniform had reached past their ankles.

They'd gravitated towards each other because of their short girl problems but then found out they had much more in common and had been friends ever since.

Zawadi turned around on the next exit and drove back to Ichigo as she remembered everything from two nights ago when she had met that sexy stranger.

CHAPTER TWO

Two nights ago

"Wear something scandalous ... and bright red lipstick," Pendo said.

She had come over at Zawadi's house and demanded she get off the bed she had not left in a week.

Since Nelson had broken up with her, Zawadi had rarely left the house and had worked from home, her staff of seven capable enough to not need her scrutiny on a daily basis.

When she was not working, she cuddled on the couch with her cat Zen and watched How To Get Away With Murder.

"You need to get over him. He is already over you," Pendo said.

Ouch, that hurt, but she needed to hear it.

Pendo went through Zawadi's closet looking past the work suits and the dinner dresses and stopped at the ratchet dresses she would sometimes buy but was never brave enough to wear.

Zawadi held her breath when Pendo picked up a see-through red dress that looked like a handkerchief.

Uh-uh, she was not wearing that. Zen came and cuddled on her lap. Good kitty—he always knew when she needed emotional support.

She dug her fingers into Zen's fur as Pendo went through the ratchet part of her wardrobe.

"Good thing you didn't cut your hair. I would have killed you if you'd cut your hair," Pendo said.

Zawadi had taken three whole years to grow her tiny weenie Afro into her long mane that fell down her back. No way was she cutting her natural hair for anyone or anything. She had spent a pretty dime on all the natural hair products and was religious about wash days and night routines.

Pendo turned around and sneered when she saw Zen on Zawadi's lap. "Put that thing down."

Zen hissed back at her. The two did not get along. Their enmity had begun when Zen had attacked Pendo's new handbag, an expensive one she had bought on a Dubai trip.

Zen had scratched at the brown leather until the inner white linen had been exposed. Zawadi didn't know why he'd done it; he had never scratched any of her bags.

Maybe Pendo's bag was made with 'mouse' leather. Why else would he scratch it? Pendo was not convinced. She said Zen was an evil cat.

Next time she had been on a trip, she had bought Zawadi an identical bag. They'd placed it where she had kept it, at the foot of the sofa, and Zen had never scratched at it. Ever. Turned out he had a personal vendetta against Pendo, and since then, the two never saw eye to eye.

Finally, Pendo picked out a hot pink bandage dress that ended mid-thigh. The sweetheart neckline plunged real low, the midriff bare.

You could not wear it with underwear—it would look tacky.

"This is the one ... This is the dress, girl!"

"No, it's not," Zawadi said.

"I'll pick you up in an hour. I have a few final errands to run." Pendo ignored her. "There are a few things I need to oversee at the shop, but then, after that, it's me and you all night."

She owned Malkia, the most sought out jewellery shop in Nairobi. She imported high-end pieces from all over the world.

"But ... I don't want to go."

"As I said, you need to get over him. He is—"

"Okay ... Okay, I'm going. You don't have to keep saying it, short lady."

Zawadi fumed, and Pendo smiled. She had gotten the reaction she'd wanted, that sleek-tongued little lady.

CHAPTER THREE

"Oh, yeah ... That's my song." Pendo dragged Zawadi back to the dance floor.

It was Wednesday, which meant ladies' night. So the deejay was taking the ladies' requests.

Zawadi stood on the dance floor. She'd said she would come, but she had made no promises about dancing. She wanted to annoy Pendo so her friend would let her go home.

Although she was a confident woman, she did not feel very assured in her hot pink dress. You could swallow one peanut and it would show in that outfit. Also, she had recently acquired stretch marks on her curvy hips.

"Hi." A tall guy with dimples smiled at Pendo. She was a sucker for dimples and immediately turned to him.

As the two flirted, Zawadi stealthily made her way back to her seat.

She leaned back on the couch and enjoyed her wine, dreaming about when she would be back in her sitting room, in her baggy sweat pants cuddling with Zen.

The deejay was playing Shaffy's 'Akabanga,' and the Rwandese hunk was going on asking his muse to come over that night.

That's when her eyes fell on the sexy stranger. He was sitting across the room staring at her.

His hungry eyes bore into her as he licked his lips. He wore a white muscle shirt and blue jeans. He was lean, not buff, and she could tell he took care of his appearance.

He was sitting with a very beautiful younger woman sporting a straight blond weave and who was trying to involve him in some sort of conversation. But he had his eyes on Zawadi. He would not take his gaze off her, and she did not want him to.

It was like everything had come to a standstill, leaving just the two of them. She sipped her wine and smiled. The young woman next to him was showing him something on her phone when he stood up.

He made his way straight towards her. She bit her lip, anxious.

"Dance with me," he said.

His voice sounded like one of those nineties R&B artists who made baby-making music.

"Sure."

As they swayed on the dance floor, she didn't hear the music—just her erratic heartbeat as they got lost in each other's eyes.

His body's heat ignited her own as they danced hip to hip. His scruffy beard sometimes grazed her neck as he leaned down to tell her how beautiful she was.

From across the room, she saw a proud Pendo who gave her a thumbs up and blew her a kiss.

Sometimes, he took the lead, and sometimes, she did. She did not even know where her dancing prowess came from. The way she moved her waist could put a belly dancer to shame, and when she ground against him and felt his hardness on her belly, she knew she was in trouble because she wanted everything he had to offer.

It was already midnight, and like Cinderella, Zawadi knew she should leave, but she didn't want to say goodbye to her sexy stranger yet. She wanted to carry him and this night with her.

She grabbed him and kissed him full on the mouth. It was a goodbye kiss, but when he tugged at the small of her back and kissed her in return, she lost it.

When he let go, they both were breathless, and it was obvious they wanted more from each other. Zawadi had never wanted anyone as much as she wanted this sexy stranger right now—she was as hot and bothered as he was.

As if reading her mind, he took her hand, and they made their way towards the exit, in haste.

CHAPTER FOUR

"Vanilla milkshake," Zawadi ordered. She had arrived at Ichigo and was waiting for Pendo.

Her friend had not yet arrived, yet her store was around the corner. Good thing she wasn't the one buying.

Zawadi thanked the waitress who promptly came back with her shake. If she'd had any appetite today, she would have ordered a whole buffet, the food here being this good. But she did not feel like eating anything.

She texted Pendo and asked her where she was. Five minutes later, and no reply. She sighed. She should have headed home.

Ten minutes later, Pendo arrived. Zawadi had only taken two sips of her milkshake, the meeting with the sexy stranger this morning still replaying on her mind, making her more miserable.

"I just had the longest day ever." Pendo yawned as she set her white purse down on the table.

"What happened?"

"Richard showed up at my store." She rolled her eyes.

Richard had been pursuing Pendo for two years, and she had been refusing his advances. He was perfect: handsome, hardworking, charming, but he had political ambitions. He wanted to run for Dagoretti's Member of Parliament, and that was a deal-breaker for Pendo.

Her mother had been a politician, and she grew up hating that life.

Pendo ordered biryani and ate as she stared at Zawadi.

Zawadi sipped her milkshake and pretended not to notice. She did not want to share. This proved too embarrassing to share.

"So what's wrong? Or do you want me to drag it out of you?"

Zawadi sighed. Fine, maybe she could tell her best friend. "I met Sexy Stranger."

"Oh my God! Really? Where?"

"Today's meeting."

She then told her everything. About what had happened that morning with the investor.

"And the strange part is that he didn't seem to recognize me. It's not like I want a ring from him, but really? He pretended he didn't know me," she said, taking a spoonful of Pendo's biryani.

Maybe she should have ordered food, too. Talking about Sexy Stranger Gerald made her hungry for many things.

"There is no way he forgot you," Pendo said. "You danced with him all night, left the club with him, and from what you told me, it was a wild night."

"I know. The meeting was just weird, and now, I'm supposed to work with him." Zawadi bit her manicured nails. She used to have the terrible habit as a child. She had stopped doing it but always regressed when she was nervous.

"Good thing is you won't get to see him daily. He is an investor"

"I got the feeling he is one of those hands-on types who micromanage everything."

Staring at him, she had wondered if perhaps he was not the one she'd kissed.

But deep down, she knew this was the man whose mouth she had tasted. Was she really that forgettable?

"So what are you going to do?" Pendo asked.

Zawadi shrugged and took another spoonful of the biryani.

"I'm going to look for another investor."

***

The next day when Zawadi woke up, she decided to get over the saga with Sexy Stranger Gerald. So what if she was forgettable? It was not the end of the world.

She sat in the living room with a bottle of coconut oil between her thighs and oiled her hair as she watched Scandal.

The house smelt like burnt Injera. She had tried to make Injera but had burnt it. Zen sat beside her watching her with sleepy green eyes. These days, he looked at her as if he didn't know what to do with her.

The doorbell rang. Zawadi frowned, not expecting anyone today. It was probably the apartments' caretaker, Mutiso, asking if he could wash her car for a fee.

"Yes?" She opened the door and came face to face with Gerald.

"Miss Zawadi."

She shivered as she remembered that voice, on that night as he'd asked her to come for him while he drove her crazy with ecstasy.

She dropped the coconut oil and put her hands across her chest. She was in old grey sweatpants and an ratty green shirt with the words 'Safaricom, The better option' written over it. To make things worse, she was not wearing a bra.

"Can I come in?" he asked.

She let him in. She didn't know how he knew where she lived and why he had come here.

Yesterday evening, she had called and told him that she was no longer interested in working together and had thanked him for the opportunity.

She had decided it was the best decision to make. She kept attracting men who had no good intentions towards her. Men like Gerald and her ex, Nelson.

She wanted to break that cycle of undeserving men in her life.

She had taken an Epsom salt bath because she had read somewhere that it cleared away negative energies. She'd wanted to cut those energetic and psychic chords deep and to form a wall of light around her aura, a wall that would keep men like Gerald away from her.

He sat on the couch, and Zen ran to his feet and flopped on his shoes.

He slightly moved his feet as if to shake Zen away. He was not a cat person, then? If he knew how choosy Zen was with people, he would appreciate this display of affection, which surprised her.

"Miss Zawadi. I didn't understand your call yesterday. I thought we had an agreement before you left my office."

His back was straight, his voice firm. Even in her house, he was power-posing her.

"My parents refused to let me buy them out," she lied.

"Bullshit. I think we have something big here, Zawadi. Many times, I see entrepreneurs self-sabotaging themselves. I think you really need to rethink your decision." He rose to leave. "Sleep over it. I want you to call me tomorrow morning, and I want you to tell me that you are ready to do business."

He'd said those last words with finality, and he towered over her and stared at her a tad too long until her cheeks heated up.

"I'll be waiting."

Zawadi showed him to the door. When she was sure he was gone, she groaned and buried her face on the cushion pillow.

Why didn't she argue back? Why didn't she confront him? He was playing her.

"Why didn't you warn me, Zen? You are supposed to be psychic. You should have told he was coming."

Zen meowed and reminded her he did not concern himself with peasant troubles, in case she forgot he was a king and she was just his mere human.

Zawadi slid down and sat on her blue fluffy carpet. Zen settled on her lap.

As bad as Gerald was for pretending, she envied his control over his emotions and how he separated work from his personal life. He was so different, and so reserved, while in work mode. The guy she'd spent that night with had been a reckless daredevil.

She needed to put her ego aside and rein in her emotions. Rolla needed an investor. She would be a fool to let this deal go. It was what her business needed.

Gerald had thrown her a lifeline by telling her to reconsider. Not many investors would have done the same.

She knew what she had to do.

CHAPTER FIVE

The next day, Zawadi decided to put her big girl pants on. She called Gerald and told him she would be delighted to work with him.

"I knew you would make the right choice."

His gruff voice over the phone aroused goose bumps on her skin.

She was going to put her ego aside for her company. Plus apart from Gerald's monetary input, he was also going to mentor and advise her.

"He is the full package," she reminded herself.

She bit her lip when she remembered his other package.

She took a walk to her local grocery shop to refill her weekly supplies. She never enjoyed a meal that lacked dhania and saumu. Also, walking cleared her mind.

She was heading back home when she spotted a familiar motorbike parked at her favourite juice bar.

She would recognize that Harley anywhere. Gerald's bike. Her pussy throbbed when she remembered their ride through the city with her legs around his waist and then later, her back on the cold leather, her legs in the sky with his tongue between her thighs.

She started walking away, but it was too late—he had already seen her and was walking towards her, his mango juice in hand.

He was not in his usual prim suit and tie like when she'd last seen him in her living room. Today, he wore a muscle shirt, and he had a cocky grin on his face which felt like it was connected to her nether regions.

"So we meet again," he said.

She put her phone into the back pocket of her jeans because her hand shook slightly. Something was different about him. She couldn't tell what exactly, but it was there.

Before she could do anything, he was next to her and kissing her on the cheek.

"You never told me your name," he said.

What was he talking about? He was in her house just yesterday.

"Ronald."

He shook her hand. His dark eyes roved over her like they had that day in the club. She wore grey sweatpants and a Puma sweater, but he looked at her as if she was queen of all that is sexy.

"Zawadi," she said.

"That's a beautiful name."

She smiled. This explained everything. They were two different people, Gerald and Sexy Stranger, Ronald. He had not forgotten her. This was good. Her ego was pleased.

"Your name is Ronald?" The fact that they were two different people excited her.

They were definitely twins, no question about that.

"Yes," he said, amused by the question. "Can I buy you a drink?"

He pointed at the juice bar.

"Sure."

This was good news. She could celebrate this with something nutritious. She ordered passion juice, and they sat down. Ronald never took his eyes off her, and she wanted to bite on that full bottom lip and scratch his back again. At this rate, they would leave here faster than they'd left the club.

"Uhm, so how do you know this place?" she asked.

"I pass by here on my way to the studio."

"Studio?"

"I'm an artist."

"That's ... great." As long as he was not an investor with a venture capital firm called Arcadia, she was fine.

"You want to see my latest painting?"

"Okay."

He took out his phone and showed her a picture of her, stark naked, lying on his bike.

She was biting her lip, her hands on her belly as she tried to hide her stretch marks.

That night when they'd left the club in heat, he had given her his overcoat, and they'd charged away from the place as if the devil had been on their trail. Her hot pink dress had ridden over her ass, and she'd been thankful for the overcoat because she had not been wearing any underwear.

Zawadi had held on tight as they'd navigated the streets of Nairobi and passed by the pedestrians, drivers, and other motorists.

She'd felt like if they knew her little secret that she was not wearing underwear.

What if they got stopped by traffic police? Oh God, she had been both scared and excited.

They'd ridden outside the city, and soon, they had been on a secluded spot in a place surrounded by beautiful pine trees. The moon had been shining bright, the stars twinkling.

She had been soaking wet.

That day, she'd wanted to be ravaged until she was sore and her body ached. Until she forgot Nelson and Kate with the blue tanzanite on her finger.

She'd wanted him to jump on her right there and then. But he'd just stood there and stared, his eyes roaming over her body.

She'd put her hands on her belly to hide some of the stretch marks.

He'd unbuttoned the overcoat, slowly, as if unwrapping his gift.

"You are perfect," he'd said and had taken her face in his hands and kissed her until all rational thought had gone out of her.

Then he'd lain her down on the bike and let his tongue do the magic.

"Oh, it's nice." Zawadi flushed as she stared at the painting.

"I have more, at my place," he said.

A tempting invitation. But she was wearing her sweatpants and on her way from the grocery store. She looked at his bike. She didn't know why she was considering it. Every time she was with him, she felt so uninhibited.

"I ..."

"I'll take you home in no time. Maybe this time, you will let me in."

Last time, he had taken her home, too, but he had dropped her at the gate. She had not let him up, and he didn't know the floor of her apartment.

"Come on, I'll make it worth your time. You won't be disappointed," he said.

Zawadi blushed. How could she say no to that? If there existed someone who never disappointed, it was Sexy Stranger Ronald.

CHAPTER SIX

"They are actually two different people," Zawadi said. She was on a call updating Pendo on the saga about Gerald and Ronald.

She yawned. She had barely slept a wink last night with Ronald. His stamina was Guinness-record-worthy, and if she had to keep up with him, she needed to go back to the gym and stay fit.

"So are they like twins?" Pendo asked.

"I think so." She had asked Ronald if he had a twin, and he had said there was no one he knew about.

The resemblance was uncanny, and she was ninety-nine percent sure they were twins.

"What if they were separated by birth?"

"You mean like in the movies?" She beeped at the Grey Toyota Harrier in front of her. She was stuck in Uhuru Highway on her way to meet Gerald.

They were signing their contract today. The money he was going to pump into Rolla would come in handy, especially since their next event was in two weeks.

"Yeah. That makes sense to me," Pendo said. She giggled and told someone on the other side of the line to stop. He was tickling her or something.

"But they would have met by now. I really don't know," Zawadi said.

"Yeah ... but Gerald just came back to the country. Wasn't he living in the Netherlands for over ten years?" Pendo asked.

That could be it. Gerald was new in town, so maybe the twins had never met each other, and it coincidentally happened that she had met both of them.

It was a perfect explanation … except her instincts screamed something was off.

Pendo moaned on the other side of the line and took a sharp intake of breath.

"Are you …?" Was she really getting it on while talking to her?

"Richard," Pendo moaned.

Zawadi switched off the phone. She was with Richard. Those two freaks were perfect for each other anyways.

Traffic eased up, and soon, she was in Westlands near Gerald's office.

She wondered if she should tell him about Ronald. If she had a twin somewhere in the world, she would want to know about it. But she also had to approach this carefully. If they had never met after all this time, it had to be because of a serious family feud, or something like that.

"Good morning, Zawadi." Gerald kissed her on the cheek as soon as she walked in.

"Morning," she said, breathless. It was difficult to think anything serious when last night, she had sat on a face that looked exactly the same.

"You came?" he asked as they sat down.

"What? Yes." God, she had to get a grip on herself.

"Let's make it official."

God, why did they have to have the same voice? Now when he said the most innocent of things, her mind would interpret them differently.

He handed her a copy of the contract. He had already signed. Zawadi scrolled down to where she was supposed to append her signature. She had already gone through the document.

She handed the papers back to him, and their fingers lightly brushed, lighting her skin on fire.

He looked at the contract and at her signature with a satisfied smile.

"Great. Now let's get to work," he said.

He had arranged for them to meet a social media marketer, one of the best reviewed in the city. He would help put Rolla more on the map.

He also said they needed to meet a web developer because her website needed a new user interface. The current one was too outdated and dull.

"I paid two hundred thousand shillings for it!" Zawadi defended her website. How could he?

"Two hundred for that free thing?" Gerald asked.

"Fr-free?"

"It's a free website. Lawrence, my web developer, will show you."

"Okay." Zawadi sulked. The guy who had built her the website had used a lot of big technical terms to assure her that he would make her a top-notch website, but the final product had been horrible, plus it always crashed.

"You have a lot to learn. Come, let's go."

They were using his sleek black BMW X6 to go to the two meetings. God, this was her dream car.

They talked about business and the economic climate of the country and the continent.

She took the moment as a chance to watch him as he drove.

Not only was he handsome, but he was smart, too. Observant and well-spoken.

He was completely her type.

But so was Ronald. Talented, spontaneous, charming, carefree, and good in bed. She bet Gerald was good in bed, too.

God, what was she thinking? She was firmly a one-man woman. She was not going to entertain these thoughts about Gerald. He would strictly be her business partner, nothing more.

After the meeting with the social media marketer who took notes on his phones and was always on his devices marketing, they met the web developer and spend the next three hours discussing some of the user interface prototypes he had.

Gerald was attentive to her as she explained what was on her mind, and he often asked her what she thought about a certain point the web developer had made. He valued her input.

She watched him as he explained something to the guy.

The fact that he was so passionate about Rolla, as much as she was, turned her on. The way he talked about Rolla's future and what her company was capable of touched her heart. Believing in her company meant he believed in her, and her vision. Not many people did.

After the meeting, they went back to the office. There were going to go through Rolla's last financial year and make projections for the next year.

"But first, we celebrate," Gerald said as he popped a bottle of Dom Pérignon and handing a glass to Zawadi. "To Rolla and to its smart, beautiful, ambitious CEO who is now my business partner. Cheers."

They clicked glasses as Zawadi internalized everything he had said. Gerald was incredible.

"Are you single?" she blurted out and regretted it as soon as the words left her mouth. It was a beautiful moment, and she did not want to ruin it. "I mean, you are perfect. Smart, hardworking. Sexy ... very sexy."

She could not stop rambling.

He was staring at her, and that mischievous glint glimmered in his eyes once more.

"I'm sorry. I—"

"You think I'm sexy."

Zawadi nodded as the Dom Pérignon caressed her tongue. She moaned. Good champagne was orgasmic to her.

He was sitting at the edge of the desk, and his gaze roamed from her heels up her legs, up the hem of her green dress, up her cleavage, settling on her lips a second too long before going back to her eyes. It was clear he was loving what he saw.

"Yes," she said. "I'm sorry. That's inappropriate."

"I'm not offended."

He smiled, and she dreamily looked at his lips over her champagne glass.

"It's not every day a beautiful woman calls me sexy."

"Really ... because I could almost swear they do. Last time during the pitch, the women were saying you could start a cult with your face and your body and that they would gladly join it. I mean, you are like perfect. Can't you see? Everywhere we went today, the women looked like they were ready to throw their soaked panties at you," she rambled on.

She looked at her wrist, the one without her watch. "I need to go. I have a meeting with the company catering food for next week's event."

"I'll walk you out."

He escorted her to the parking lot and held the door for her as she got in.

"Gerald, I'm sorry about everything I said. I would hate to sabotage our partnership before it started. Because Rolla needs you." Her eyes fell.

"No need to explain. I love it when a woman speaks her mind." He kissed her goodbye on the cheek before she got into her car. "See you tomorrow, Zawadi."

"Bye," she whispered before she drove away.

As she left Lang'ata Road on her way to her apartment in Karen, her mind wandered back to Gerald. He was charming, charismatic, and with a hint of being dark, just the way she liked her men.

She liked him.

This complicated things because she liked Ronald, too.

Speaking of which, she had to get to the bottom of this. Why didn't they know of each other, and why was she the only one who knew of this? She needed to reunite them. Which is why she had to rein in her feelings and take things slow with both of them.

Since she had crossed the line with Ronald, she definitely should not cross it with Gerald.

She pouted. That would have been fun. Ronald took her to the stars. She'd bet Gerald could take her to the moon and beyond. He was so attentive. He would be an incredible lover—he would be thorough as he pleased her.

But she would never know, because she would never cross that line. Then, she remembered he had not told her if he was single.

Was he?

CHAPTER SEVEN

Someone was ringing her doorbell. Zawadi groaned. It was six in the morning, and she had just got home. Rolla's event of the month had just happened in Machakos. It had been a success, but she had been up all night.

Today, she just wanted to sleep. The doorbell rang again. She dragged her feet into her slippers and went to the door with half-closed eyes.

"Angel."

Her ex, Nelson, was standing there with cream roses in his hand and a smile that once used to make her weak. She was definitely dreaming this. She closed the door in his face and went back to sleep. She must be so tired to dream about him.

She immediately fell into deep sleep until the doorbell rang again.

She decided to ignore it, but it persisted. She cursed. If it was Nelson, she was going to tell him to crawl back to Hell.

Luckily, it was Gerald. She smiled and wished she had washed her face or put on some lip gloss.

"'Morning," she said.

Something was wrong, though. His creased shirt was unbuttoned, his tie in his pocket. She had never seen him so untidy before. He still wore the same suit from yesterday.

"Are you okay?" When he'd left the day before, he had been fine.

Zawadi had thought she would use the event to introduce the twins to each other, but Gerald had left early and Ronald had arrived late. They never got to meet.

Gerald closed the door behind them and pinned her against the panel. He started kissing her neck. She had been dreaming about this, but he was too intense, too demanding. And something felt off.

She pushed him away from her. He stared at her, confused.

"Don't you want me? You always want me," he said.

Always? First of all, she had never been intimate with him. Only with Ronald.

"I only want to give you pleasure. I want you, Zawadi. I need you."

This was too crazy to imagine. She realized that his eyes flashed from pitch black to honey brown. She had never seen eye contacts like the ones he was wearing before.

One minute, he looked like Gerald, and the next like …

"R … Ronald?" she called him.

He did not hear her. Although he was staring at her, he seemed lost in his own world. It seemed that his mind was in some sort of conflict.

"I won't let him take you away from me. You are mine, Zawadi … my precious gift."

Zawadi was Swahili for gift, and Ronald had always called her his precious gift. How did Gerald know that?

"Don't listen to Ronald. Ever since you walked into my office, I knew you were the woman for me. You are the one I want to build an empire with, conquer the world with, and live my life with, Zawadi. You are fucking everything. You are perfect."

Wait, what? He was spouting so much nonsense right then ...

"You are mine, Zawadi. Gerald doesn't love you like I do."

What on Earth ... So they knew each other?

He leaned in to kiss her, and she slapped him hard across the face, not knowing which man she was dealing with here. Her head was reeling, her whole body shaking.

"Zawadi ..." He reached for her again.

"Stay away from me!"

She pushed him away and started running towards the kitchen. He followed behind, asking her to stop.

She reached for a knife and put it between them.

"Don't come any closer."

He looked at the sharp blade between them and her shaking hand. Disappointment, betrayal, and anger flashed on his face in a millisecond. Then he started breathing hard. He let out a wounded animal cry and put his hands on his head, as if in pain.

"Gerald?" Zawadi called. He did not hear her.

He fell on his knees and howled.

His shirt was soaked in sweat, and the veins on his neck looked like they would burst.

She took a step forward, her knife still in hand. Tears were falling down her face. This was utter madness.

"G-Gerald?" she called.

He went quiet and stopped panting. He removed his hands from his head and took a deep breath. Then he stood up. His left eye was black, his right brown.

"You have to choose, Zawadi. Him, or me?"

"What?"

How could she choose? And what was he on about?

Then, he clenched his fist and punched himself. Zawadi screamed and ran to the other side of the room, far away from him. He was punching himself and arguing with himself.

It sounded like two people having a row and fighting. But how could it, since there was just one man in her living room? What was this drama?

"She is mine!"

"Stay away from her, you piece of shit!"

"You don't get to tell me what to do!"

"I made you!"

"And I saved you!"

He turned to her. His face was bruised, and he had bled on her blue carpet. She was shaking hard and felt faint. What was going on here?

"Zawadi ..."

"Don't touch me."

He looked so different and wild and dangerous and insane.

"Don't be scared. We just want you to choose. Him, or me?"

"We?" Zawadi asked.

"It's me you want." Their eyes met.

Invisible hands closed on her throat, feeling too tight, as he kept on watching her with that intense, expectant gaze.

"Go away ... please," she pleaded, but his eyes stayed focused on her, like he couldn't hear her.

"Tell him it's me you want." His eyes had gone dark, and she knew it was Ronald.

It was clear to her by now that they were not twins. Gerald and Ronald were both one very sick and dangerous man. She had been stupid, and she had been played, and now, her life was in danger.

"We are so good together. Give us a chance," brown-eyed Gerald said.

He was the less impulsive one, so Zawadi knew that if she were to get out of this, she had to reason with him.

"Can I please think about this? Please, Gerald?"

His eyes softened. Then, they turned black. "Ronald, please."

He broke eye contact then, and she took in a sharp breath.

"Tomorrow. Make your decision by tomorrow." He smiled.

"Okay ... Just ... just give me some time alone today, please."

This was too much; her knees gave in. She sank to the floor. She remained powerless to do anything as he carried her to the sofa and gently placed her there, the knife frozen in her grip.

"Are you okay?" He caressed her chin.

"I'm fine. Please give me space," she said.

He seemed hesitant, and she worried he would not leave. She could still use the knife. But maybe appealing to reason could still work.

"Please, I need some time alone."

He nodded, kissed her one last time, and left. When she heard his footsteps going down the stairs, she quickly ran to the door and locked it.

She sat back on the couch and sobbed. It had been too good to be true. She should have known.

She reached for her phone and told Pendo to come for her. She did not trust herself to drive—she was quaking like a leaf.

She then ran up to her room and reached for an overnight bag and packed a few of her clothes.

She didn't know which ones she took. She just stuffed them into the bag together with her work laptop and put Zen in his cage, which he hated, but she didn't have time for that right now.

Today was a day from Hell. First Nelson, and then Gerald-Ronald? She sobbed as she remembered her encounter with him.

Her doorbell rang, and she froze. Was he back? She peeped at the keyhole, and down there stood Pendo. Never had she been so glad to see her friend. She opened the door and flung her arms around her.

"What happened? Who do I need to kill?"

"Nelson, and then Gerald who is Ronald. Oh, God," Zawadi sobbed.

"Calm down and tell me everything. Deep breaths," Pendo instructed.

Zawadi's sobs subsided.

"Nelson was here in the morning with roses ... and then Gerald came. Turns out he is Ronald, too—"

"What?"

"He is both of them. He is sick."

She explained everything that had happened, how Gerald had fought with himself and argued with himself and told her to choose between him and Ronald and that she had told him she would decide by tomorrow.

"This is messed up. We have to leave before he comes back," Pendo said.

They called Mutiso, the caretaker, and asked him to check for any suspicious people or cars downstairs. The dutiful man said no. They quickly got into Pendo's Mazda Demio and drove off.

Zawadi was sobbing all the way 'til they arrived in Roysambu where Pendo lived in a two-bedroom bungalow. Her friend led her to the guest room which she had used many times before, and she crashed on the bed.

"You can sleep all you want today. Give me any instructions you have, and I'll call your office and let them know."

"Thank you."

Zawadi fell asleep, but even in her dream, he was there. She was in Ronald's apartment. Naked in his bed, in post-coital bliss. He was snoring next to her.

She was feeling thirsty. Their sex marathon had drained her. She reached for his white muscle shirt and wore it. She loved that it smelled like him. She tiptoed out of bed and walked downstairs to the kitchen.

The fridge door was ajar, something red dripping from it. Blood was all over the kitchen floor. She walked closer and looked.

There was a head in the fridge. Not just any head, but hers.

She screamed and took two steps back. Ronald and Gerald were standing behind her with smiles on their faces.

She ran out of the house, still screaming, and they ran after her, laughing. She fell down and closed her eyes as they circled around her.

She woke up, drenched in sweat, back to reality which was also a nightmare. Murphy's Law was in full effect. Everything that could go wrong had indeed gone wrong.

She cried over the whole thing, how easily she had fallen for Ronald, the chance she would never get with Gerald, and the crazy voice in her head that said it was already too late because she was in love with the man.

CHAPTER EIGHT

The next week was a blur for Zawadi. She worked from home and rarely left Pendo's house. She blocked Gerald-Ronald's numbers as well as Nelson's. He was calling and texting her saying how sorry he was and that he needed to talk.

She was paranoid about everyone and everything. Pendo proved a very supportive friend. Even while she was at work, she checked in with Zawadi every hour.

Zawadi barely slept. For the first time in her life, she considered taking sleeping pills, but then she did not want to knock herself out, in case he showed up. Luckily, he never did.

Why did the interesting ones have to be crazy, anyway?

On Sunday morning, she was in the kitchen watching Pendo make pancakes and talk about how annoying Richard was.

Zen was in the corner of the room drinking milk from a bowl that Pendo had bought for him. Zawadi had forgotten to carry his food and his bowls.

These days, he never hissed at Pendo and even lay at her feet sometimes. It seemed as if he had gotten over his beef with her after she'd taken him and his broken human in.

The doorbell rang. Zawadi and Pendo stopped talking and stared at each other. Pendo cautiously went to the door with a ladle in hand and peered through the key hole.

Zawadi followed behind with a pan in hand.

"Who is it?" she whispered.

Pendo nodded, telling her to put the pan down. She opened the door, and Nelson stood there in his blue suit, similar to the one he'd worn on the day he'd broken up with her and told her he was moving back to Durban.

Zawadi frowned at Pendo, who had been saying maybe she should hear what he had to say. This way, she would get her closure.

She wondered if maybe there was a crack in Hell and all the ghosts of the men in her life were showing up to haunt her.

Or maybe it was Heaven's doing. The angels and their perfect choir were not entertaining enough for everyone, and so they had decided to turn her life into a joke to amuse themselves.

"Hi, Angel." He smiled. Today, he carried pink roses.

"I don't want to see you ever again," she said.

"Let me explain. I made a mistake, Angel—"

Zawadi closed the door in his face. She was furious at Pendo for opening it in the first place.

"You need to hear him out," Pendo explained.

Zawadi rolled her eyes and took her breakfast. She ate five pancakes and drank three cups of coffee. She could feel blood and adrenaline pumping in her veins.

"I don't need his bullshit right now. You of all people know that."

"Okay, I'm sorry I overstepped," Pendo said. Then she burst out laughing. "Did you see his face when you slammed the door on him?"

"Please, Angel," Zawadi said, imitating Nelson's voice, and they burst out laughing. She laughed until her ribs hurt.

"He is crazier than Gerald-Ronald. He proposed to Kate two weeks ago, and now, he is back with pink roses wanting to get back together."

"My taste in men is messed up," Zawadi said, and they laughed at her fucked-up life.

It turned out to be the best therapy she needed.

CHAPTER NINE

The next day, Zawadi decided to go back to her house. She was not going to avoid Gerald-Ronald forever. She had a business relationship with him, one she was figuring out how to dissolve.

She had called him up.

"Hello?" His voice had been raspy, and he'd sounded tired.

"I want to meet you tomorrow at eight. At your office," she'd said.

"Okay. Zawadi—"

She had ended the phone call before he could talk more.

She packed her overnight bag and put Zen in a cage, ready to leave. She would drop her luggage at her apartment and then go to Gerald's office.

She opened Pendo's front door and found Nelson standing on the other side.

"Angel."

He looked cold, his coat wet since it was drizzling. She wondered how long he had been there.

She sighed. "You have five minutes, Nelson."

"I was wrong to leave, Zawadi."

"Three minutes."

"You want the truth? Okay, I'll tell you the truth, Angel. I fell in love with you, but I always wondered how my life would have turned out if I was with her. I needed to make sure. So I went to her, but then I realized it's you I want ... and that's why I came back ... That's the truth. It's over between me and her."

He looked at her as if he expected her to clap for him.

As far as Zawadi was concerned, Nelson was the worst of the men in her life.

He had ended their three-year relationship and run off to his ex who had dumped him when he'd once become bankrupt in a business deal gone wrong.

That's the same woman he had left her for.

The sex with Kate had probably been good on that first day when he'd arrived back in Durban before she asked him to buy her ten Gucci bags and take her to Paris for dinner. Nelson was stingy with his money.

Zawadi had stalked Kate's social media and realized she was a high-maintenance woman. Not that there was anything wrong with that, but knowing Nelson, she knew he could not keep up with her.

This was the same man who booked two-star hotels when he travelled to make business deals worth millions of shillings.

Right there and then, Nelson went down on his knees before her. He brought out the blue velvet box. He opened it and of course, inside was the damned blue tanzanite ring.

"What are you doing?"

"I am showing you that I am sure, Angel. This time, I am sure. It's you I want. It's you I want in my life. Will you marry me?"

A month ago, Zawadi would have jumped on him and screamed yes. She would have said yes before he even asked. Now, this gesture and those sweet words meant nothing to her. She didn't feel a thing for him. Pendo was right about closure. This moment right here confirmed that she was over him.

Her heart was with someone else. Someone who was two and one at the same time, and she needed to get to the bottom of this. She needed to talk to Gerald-Ronald. She needed to see him and know if he was okay.

She would demand that he tell her the whole truth about who he was.

Her Uber arrived.

Zawadi walked past Nelson who was still on his knees and ran to the car.

CHAPTER TEN

Zawadi left Zen and her overnight bag in the Uber and told the driver to wait for her.

"Is he in?" she asked Janice soon as she walked inside Arcadia.

"Yes. But ..."

She started walking towards Gerald's office.

He stood up when she opened the door, still as handsome as she remembered. Today, he wore a blue suit, and he had dark circles under his eyes. He looked like he had not slept in a long time.

"What are you?" she asked.

"Zawadi—"

"I liked you, and I trusted you. Both of you" She could not believe she was saying that. "At least, I deserve to know the truth."

He took a step, and she took one back. He stopped.

"Have a seat." He invited her to sit, and he went back to his executive chair.

"Are you sure you want to know?"

"Yes" she whispered. She needed to know.

He was silent for a minute, his sad eyes flashing from brown to black, waiting to see her reaction. She was cautious and a little afraid, but her curiosity and her stupid feelings for him superseded everything. She stayed stuck to her seat.

His eyes flashed back to brown again. Then, he proceeded and told her the story of his life.

***

He was born in Lamu, Kenya as Gerald Mwamburi. His father was in textile import business, his mother a housewife. He was an only child.

"They wanted me to be the best I could be."

Sloppiness was not allowed, and neither was slacking behind in class. He just could not become the second in his class. Scoring a ninety-five in a test was the worst thing he could do.

He tried all he could to please them, but his father was a hard man. He would whip him every second he got, for the smallest of mistakes. For thinking and acting like a normal child.

Then one day, after a rough beating from his father for scoring eighty in his geography exam, he woke up in a hospital bed.

He had a couple of broken ribs. One eye was shut, his left hand sprained. There were drips attached to his body and a nurse checking his vitals. His mother sat curled up in a chair, crying.

His father stood beside her, hands on her shoulders as he comforted her.

Gerald felt a cold sweat all over his body. He wished she would stop crying, first because he didn't like seeing her cry, and second because his father would deal with him for making her cry.

He was drifting in and out of consciousness, afraid, when he heard a voice inside him. It said it was going to help him.

The voice said his name was Ronald, and he was going to protect him from then on.

"And he did."

When Gerald returned home from the hospital, he resumed his normal life. His father was still abusive.

He would stay in and study, do his homework, iron his clothes, and remain a perfect child. From his room, he could hear the kids who lived in their neighbourhood playing football, and he would wish he was out with them.

That's when Ronald would take over. He would help Gerald climb down the window and sneak out, play football, then go back to the room.

Ronald did what Gerald couldn't do—he was brave and cunning and known for picking fights.

"One day, the principal at my primary school summoned my parents because of a fight Ronald had. My mother would not believe it; she said I was a good boy. My father said the same thing."

"The principal told them they were wrong. That I had been in a fight with one of the kids in my class. He told them I had scraped my left knee and the school nurse had bandaged it up. He told me to show my parents my left knee. I did—there was no bandage and no wound.

Ronald was the one who was hurt, and right there in the office was me, Gerald."

His eyes flashed from brown to black, and Zawadi shivered.

"From that day, I knew I could do anything. I became the good son my parents wanted me to be, and Ronald helped me experience life the way I wanted to."

He had been like that all through his teenage years up to now. He was both the nerd and the popular kid at school.

"I have split personality, Zawadi. The one you met at the club was Ronald, and the one you met at the office was me, Gerald. I asked Ronald to stay away from you, but he wouldn't listen. He said he was falling in love. I told him I was falling in love, too. It

… it has never happened before. We have never been in love with the same person before.

"It caused me to have a breakdown, and that's what you saw happen that day I came to your house. I'm so sorry for everything, Zawadi. You deserve better from me and from any man. You are perfect. That day after I left, I drove straight to my therapist. I have been going again since then."

Zawadi nodded. This was something you saw on TV or read in a book; it never happened in real life. Yet, here she was, with feelings for a man with two personalities, and he was not the villain in this story, after all. To experience what he did as a kid could have broken anyone.

A tear rolled down her face because she didn't know what to do. She was still a little frightened of him, but she wanted to hug him, too. She wanted to be there for him.

"I'm sorry," she said. "So what do we do now? I want to help."

He looked at her, as if astonished that she had not already run out. "You want to help?"

"Yes."

"Well, my therapist asked to meet you. I told her you would never agree to it."

"We can go, yes." She wanted to know more about this split personality condition and to help him in any way she could.

"You are very brave, Miss Zawadi."

He smiled a slow smile, and she eyed his full lips.

She rose from her seat. "I have to go. My cat Zen is in the car; he is very grumpy. You will let me know when your therapist wants to meet, yes? And thank you for telling me your story."

He stood up slowly in a way that was non-threatening. She was surprised that she did not flinch. But her knees grew weak and her mouth went dry. He was still as tantalizing as ever.

He took her hand and gave it a light kiss. "Thank you."

Then, he kissed her forehead, and she leaned against his chest as they hugged.

"Bye," she said.

"See you soon." His voice was a low purr, and his eyes flashed from brown to black again.

CHAPTER ELEVEN

One year later
February 14th, 2019
"Auntie Zawadi has a big tummy," Riziki, Pendo's nephew, said.

He put his hand on Zawadi's swollen belly and left a wet print on her white dress.

"Did you swallow a big yam, Aunt Zawadi?" he asked as he took another sip of his milk. The curious little inquisitor was very interested in understanding this big belly phenomenon.

Zawadi laughed. Pendo and Richard joined in. They were sitting next to her at the dining table, holding hands. They had just come back from their honeymoon in the Maldives.

Riziki's mom, Neema, was in the kitchen stealthily adding carrots to his juice. Riziki hated carrots.

They were all at Pendo's house. Valentine's Day marked her mother's death anniversary. She had passed on this day in 2010 from ovarian cancer, and they gathered here every year to celebrate her life.

"Yes, I swallowed a big yam."

"Was it big like this?" Riziki asked, his little arms extended as far as they could go.

"I think it was bigger than that, buddy," Zawadi said.

Riziki prodded her tummy lightly to feel how big the yam was.

Gerald walked from the kitchen with a plate of oranges and put them before her.

She cooed when she saw them. These days, she basically survived on oranges. She ate them all the time, even in the middle of the night.

"Uncle Gerald, Auntie Zawadi swallowed a big big yam," Riziki said.

"I noticed."

Gerald winked at Zawadi who was already eating her oranges. He put his hand on her tummy where their two sons were growing. They should be here any day now.

A year ago after Gerald had told her the truth about his split personality, Zawadi had decided to get involved and help him in any way she could, because she had feelings for him.

They had started going to therapy, and they were still going. Gerald had his own private sessions, too, and lately, his parents had agreed to go with him once a week. It was doing him good.

Therapy had also helped Zawadi's relationship with her mother and her only brother Mwamba become better.

During that time, it had become clear that she and Gerald were both in love with each other, so they had remained friends and lovers. They did business together and rode on his motorbike at night. They had arguments like any other couple and then had steamy make up sex afterwards, and then, they had made babies. Two babies who would be arriving in the world any day now.

At first, Gerald had been concerned when he'd heard that the boys were twins, but then, Zawadi had assured him they would end up fine because they had him as a father.

He was going to be a great dad. He was not going to be anything like his father. He was a good man. The boys would grow up smart and healthy.

"Who do you think the babies will look like?" Richard asked Pendo.

"Me, of course," Zawadi and Gerald replied at the same time.

***

That night when they got home, Zawadi was tired, and her feet were swollen. Gerald helped her take off her sandals as soon as they closed the door.

They had bought a three-bedroom mansion with a garden in Kilimani. They had loved this house because it was homely and the neighbourhood was safe and secure, and they'd both felt it was somewhere they could raise a family in.

"What's that?" she asked as she felt something soft under her foot. There were red roses all over the floor.

"I thought girls love flowers on Valentine's Day."

Zawadi giggled. She didn't feel very much like a girl but like a bloated watermelon. She had gained over twenty kilos over the course of nine months.

As if reading her mind, Gerald kissed her on both cheeks and then on the mouth. "You are the most beautiful woman I know."

Then, he went down on his knees, and she gasped. He opened a white box and brought out a beautiful red ruby ring. A tear fell down from her eyes, and Gerald's were misty.

"Zawadi ... you are my heart and my soul. You loved me when I didn't love myself and you accept me as I am. You are the light in my life, and you are the best thing that has ever happened to me.

"Every day, I pray that I may find more ways to show you that I love you. I want to spend my whole life with you, raise a family with you, and grow old with you. Zawadi Juma, will you do me the honour of becoming my wife?"

"Yes," she whispered as tears ran down her cheeks.

He put the ring on her finger, and she pulled him up and gave him a kiss.

In the background, their favourite song, 'Burinde Bucya' by Meddy, was playing—Ikinyarwanda for 'until morning.'

When they'd started dating, Gerald had been paranoid that she would one day change her mind and leave him. It had been a dark time for both of them.

They would fight and then fuck and then he would ask her to stay the night.

"If you are going to leave me, then at least stay with me until morning," he would urge her.

"I am not going anywhere," she would say.

They would lie back down on the bed and make sweet love again. Gerald would beg her to never leave. It was during one of those nights that their babies had been conceived.

"I'm going to be a great husband, I promise." He kissed the ring on her finger, and his eyes flashed from black to brown.

Pendo had said she was a lucky girl who got to have the best of both worlds, and she was right. Gerald was amazing, and she was honoured to become his wife.

They were dancing slow and whispering naughty things when she felt a warm liquid gushing between her legs. She looked down at the wet floor.

"I think my water broke," she said, looking at the moisture drenching her thighs.

"Oh, are you sure?" Gerald froze, and his eyes grew big.

Zawadi laughed—he was more scared than she was.

"Yes, I'm sure. Go get the bag."

"Okay." He ran back to the bedroom and came out with her maternity bag which they had packed a week before. He looked like the one who was going to give birth.

"Let's go," he said.

"Relax. It's not that—" The words were cut by a sharp pain in her belly, the worst she had ever felt in her life.

"Mother Flower, let's go!" she yelled. She forgot everything she had learnt on YouTube about how to breathe while in labour. She had watched extraordinarily brave women have water births at home all by themselves and thought it would be a walk in the park. She'd been so wrong!

***

Four hours later, Gerald and Zawadi welcomed Baraka and Bakari, the twins, into the world. They kissed and hugged and stared at their two bundles of joy with awe.

Valentine's Day would now always be a very special day in their lives. On this day, they would celebrate the love they felt for each other and the gifts of that love, their two sons.

MUKAMI NGARI

Mukami Ngari is from Nairobi, Kenya.

She is the author of the critically acclaimed novel, Pharaoh's Bed.

She enjoys telling sweet passionate romance and women fiction stories set in Africa. When she is not writing or reading, she enjoys practicing yoga and watching supernatural T. V shows.

Follow her on her social media account to connect with her and to find out about new releases.

Twitter: https://twitter.com/mukami_ngari

OTHER BOOKS BY LOVE AFRICA PRESS

Unravelling His Mark by Zee Monodee

Series: The Protectors #2

Genre: Romantic Suspense

BLURB

A man with a mission

A year earlier, a mutiny broke inside the ranks of the clandestine Corpus Agency. Only one loose thread remains to be apprehended: an assassin named Evangeline. When intel from an asset points to a woman in Mauritius who could be her, Zachariah Hashemi, a mixed race Muslim from Tanzania, is tasked with bringing the renegade to justice...aka a swift death.

A woman with nothing to hide

French-Mauritian PR maven Annabelle de Castelban is throwing all she has into making her communications agency a success. When an opportunity to partner with a renowned international firm knocks on her door, she jumps on it, even if it means she has to fight her attraction to the devastatingly handsome man and the sizzling chemistry sparking between them.

A killer with a plan

Annabelle has no idea Zach is here to determine if she is a mercenary with no remorse. And the more he gets to know her, the more it becomes obvious she cannot be this twisted assassin. Indeed, Evangeline is near, and when Zach finds out Annabelle is the killer's latest target, he will stop at nothing to protect the woman he has in the meantime fallen in love with.

As they race against the clock, will they both be able to thwart the psychopath's plan to kill them in the most devious way?

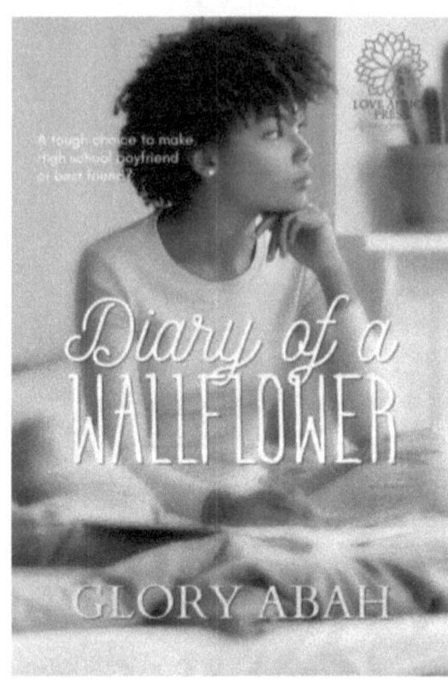

Diary of a Wallflower by Glory Abah
Genre: New Adult Contemporary Romance
BLURB:
I have always been a wallflower—too quiet, too shy, with a boring life that revolves only around work and church.

But boring is about to get a twist: Alex, my high school boyfriend, pops back into my life, though he hardly seems to recognise me and appears to like my friend, Chioma. And Simon, my best friend? Seems he has feelings for me!

Did I mention I might still be in love with Alex?

Suddenly, I am thrust into a daunting love triangle … Two choices lie before me: best friend or high school boyfriend?

Do I bury my head in the sand and go for my best friend? Or do I fight for my ex, for a love that was always meant to be, it appears?

What would a wallflower do?

Pharaoh's Bed by
Mukami Ngari
Series: Nubia Love #1
Genre: Historical
Romance

BLURB:
Maa's dreams come true
when the prince of
Aksum chooses her to be
his bride. However on
the night of their
marriage ceremony, the
evil Pharaoh Lamani of
Kemet invades Aksum
with his army. He takes the throne and Maa as his
concubine.

She should hate him, but each time their eyes meet it
feels like she has known him all her life. Like the
hauntingly beautiful Lamani should be hers.

Can she love someone who ruins everything she
cherishes?

Find out more and sign up for LAP book news:
www.loveafricapress.com/newsletter